Shatter
Gnat Smoke Press
Aug 2, 2021

gnat smoke

1

SHATTER

by John Ryland

This story is for Madison.

The First Chapter

"Who is that?" Damon asked, pointing to the thin red-haired girl methodically picking her way through the crowd in front of Providence High School. She moved along the sidewalk timidly, coming toward them. He and his friends had garnered the coveted spot outside the entrance to the freshman hall: front corner of the expansive landing at the top of the stairs. They had a perfect view of the sidewalks in both directions and could watch everyone as they made their way into the school. From here, no freshman would escape their prying eyes.

"Dude." Easton Brooks laughed, draping an arm across Damon's shoulders. "No. Don't even go there."

"What?" Damon asked, shrugging as he watched the girl approach. "She's kinda cute." Something stirred within him that he couldn't explain, a desire to get to know her better.

She was tall and thin, but not skinny. Her auburn hair had been swept to the side, hanging over one shoulder. Her fair skin was smooth and creamy, highlighting a pair of thin, pink lips that turned down slightly in the corners of her mouth.

She moved carefully, avoiding contact with her classmates, most of whom ignored her, but there was a certain gracefulness to the way she slid in and out of the crowd.

Even from a distance, he could tell that there was something about her that was different from the other girls he'd seen. There was something in the way she moved, the way she observed everyone around her. There was a vulnerability to her, but with a hint of defiance.

So far, the sampling of the freshmen he'd seen, told him that more than half of the girls in his class would be blonde. Dark black hair was the next popular, though most of them added bright red lipstick for a splash of color to let people know they weren't goth. Natural brown made up most of the rest, with a smattering of various dyed colors like blue or green.

The girl picking her way through the crowd was only the second natural-looking redhead he'd seen. His eyes followed her, the beginnings of a smile tugging at the corners of his mouth.

"Okay, I'll cut you some slack since you're new here and it's the first day of school. That-" Easton pointed at the girl "- is Tamira Brannigan. She's a weird, freaky little thing that you want to avoid at all costs. I know you're desperate, but don't even go there. It's just not worth it, man."

"First of all, I'm not desperate," Damon replied, shrugging Easton's arm off his shoulders. His friends shared a laugh at his expense, but he barely heard them. "Anyway, what's wrong with her?"

He watched as Tamira smoothly dodged a heavy-set boy tossing a football into the air. She darted around another girl who had stopped in the middle of the sidewalk to finish the text on her phone. The red-haired girl eyed her suspiciously as she passed.

"Dude. Today is the first day of our first year in high school. Don't do something that will tarnish your reputation for the next four years. Even talking to Tamira Brannigan could do that. She's hella-weird, man."

"Really?" Damon asked with a grin. "Hella-weird? Really?"

"He's not wrong," Brady added from his perch atop the wide concrete railing that lined the platform and steps. Like many of the girls, he had light blond hair that he kept brushed back in a pompadour wave. "She's like super careful not to touch anything. *Any*-thing. Or anyone. It's like she's afraid of catching something."

Damon's brow furrowed with curiosity. "Why?" he asked.

"Did you miss the part about her being weird?" Easton asked shaking his head.

"Come on, man." Damon watched the girl skirt the massive concrete newel post at the bottom of the steps, giving it a wide berth. She started up the steps, taking each one in a slow, methodical march as other students streamed around her.

"Watch this." Brady slid off the rail and positioned himself in Tamira's path. When she made the landing at the top, he jumped toward her, yelling "Watch out!"

Tamira threw her hands up in front of her face, dropping the binders she'd been clutching to her chest. She let out a scared yelp and shrank away from Brady. Damon shook his head, watching the rest of the surrounding students laugh as they moved past her without offering to help.

"Man, you're a real jerk. Do you know that?" Damon pushed past his laughing friend and went to the girl who'd squatted to pick up her belongings. She pulled back from him as he kneeled beside her.

"What do you want?" she asked.

Damon froze, his face inches from hers. His breath caught in his throat as he stared, captivated, into her big green eyes. They darted around his face, sparkling in the morning light.

When they finally met his, Damon offered a smile. "Hey."

She dropped her gaze quickly, offering a whispered, "Hey," in return.

"I'm sorry about that. Brady's just a jerk." Damon picked up a red binder and held it out to her, still smiling. "I think this is yours."

Tamira looked up, her eyes on his, and her expression softened. A smile almost escaped her lips. "Uh, thanks." She took the binder and stood as the last of the students filed into the school around them.

"I'm Damon Kennedy. It's nice to meet you."

Tamira looked at him then dropped her gaze again as they stood close. "Me too. Uh. I mean it's nice to meet you too. I'm Tamira Brannigan." She sighed, watching the students disappear into the school. "But I'm sure you already know that." She looked everywhere but at Damon as she pushed a lock of long red hair behind her ear.

"How would I know you? We just met. Are you famous?" he asked with a grin.

A soft laugh escaped her. "Not hardly. I'm sure your buddies will fill you in. If they haven't already." An internal shudder ran through her as she spared him another glance and found his eyes. They were deep and brown and seemed to be looking into her rather than at her.

"I'm new here." Damon shoved his fingers into the pockets of his jeans and shrugged. "Nice to meet you."

She fought a smile. "You already said that, but it's nice to meet you too, again, Damon Kennedy." She watched a smile pull one side of his mouth slightly higher than the other as his head tilted just a few degrees to his left. She looked away, taking in a long breath to calm the flutter in her chest. This was the longest conversation she'd had with a boy in years, and he was gorgeous.

Damon ran a hand over his crop of wavy brown hair. "So, maybe I'll see you around?"

Tamira flashed him a brief smile and nodded sheepishly. "Probably so. We do go to the same school." She started into the door, but he reached out and put a hand on her arm.

"Wait."

Tamira stopped suddenly. Her head snapped around, finishing with a flourish of red hair that landed on her shoulder. Her wide eyes fell on his hand, then she looked up at him in shock.

Reading her reaction, he pulled his hand away and shoved it back into the pocket of his jeans. "Sorry."

Tamira's face softened as she stared at him. She shook her head and sighed. "Look, you don't have to do this."

"Do what?"

"You said you're new. If your jerk friends put you up to this, you don't have to do it."

Damon shook his head, confused. "Nobody put me up to anything."

A sardonic smile crept to her lips. "Okay. Whatever." She walked through the doors, leaving him alone on the platform as the first bell rang, calling all students to class.

Damon threw his hands in the air and let them drop. Shaking his head, he walked into Providence High School for the first time.

"Mind if I sit here?"

Tamira startled slightly when Damon spoke, then slowly looked up from the book in front of her. Her eyes grew wide for an instant, and a soft gasp escaped her when she saw him. Her eyes lingered on his for a moment, then she looked back down, collecting herself.

Although she knew better, she hadn't been able to chase the image of him from her mind all morning. "You again?" she asked, trying not to sound happy.

"So, can I sit down?"

"If you want," she replied, almost in a whisper. She cleared her throat and turned the page in her book just to have something to do with her hands.

"I'm Damon Kennedy, remember? From this morning."

Her eyes narrowed slightly as she looked at him. "Why do you do that?"

"Do what?"

"Introduce yourself with your first and last name? It makes you sound like a politician."

Damon laughed. "I don't know. I'm new here. I guess I just want people to know my name."

She shrugged. "Okay Damon Kennedy, sit where you want. It's a free country." She went back to her reading, consciously keeping her breathing calm despite her racing heart.

Damon watched her for a moment. She was almost as tall as him, but sitting here, slumped over her book, with her shoulders drawn in, she looked half the size she did this morning. That is probably the idea, he thought. The smaller she was the less likely she was to be seen.

Tamira glanced up from her book, catching him staring at her. Her eyes washed over his hair. It was slightly disheveled like he'd been running his hands through it. It wasn't long, but collar length, with a crop of natural curls at the ends. It looked like the kind of hair that would be fun to run your fingers through.

He was looking at her with a hint of a smile on his lips. When she met his gaze, her heart wanted to flutter, but she wouldn't let it.

"Yes?" she asked. "Is something wrong?"

Damon cleared his throat, looking away as he scratched the side of his neck. His cheeks flushed lightly, having been caught staring. "I, uh, just saw an empty seat. Is it okay?"

Tamira sighed and looked at the empty chairs along both sides of the table she sat at. She placed the bookmark between the pages of her book and closed it. "Sit down before you make a scene, Damon Kennedy." She watched him slide into a seat across from her. "Don't you and your friends talk?"

"Yeah, sure. I guess. Why?"

"Then I'm sure they've filled you in."

"Filled me in?" Damon asked. Of course, they had. They'd spent all morning "filling him in" about Tamira Brannigan. She was weird. She didn't have any friends. She went straight home after school and didn't socialize. She didn't have *any* social media accounts. There was a rumor that she didn't even have a cell phone.

She gave him a patronizing smile. "Then I'm sure they've told you I'm weird and to stay away from me."

"So?" he shrugged. "What if they did?"

Tamira looked at him, her green eyes searching his face. "And?"

"And what?"

"Why are you here?" she asked, interlacing her fingers atop the book.

Damon smiled, tossing one hand into the air. "Because my dad got a job here. Legally they couldn't leave me behind, so I had to come with them."

She let out an incredulous chuckle. "Not here, in town. Genius. Here, as in at this table?"

Damon shrugged. "Oh. I had to sit somewhere, and this seat was open. Is it a crime?"

A sarcastic chuckle escaped her as she shook her head. "To a lot of people, it would be considered one. A social crime anyway." She started gathering her things. "I'll do you a favor, okay? I'm the weird girl. People don't like me, and I've made my peace with it. It's just how things are. Somebody's got to be the social pariah and I guess I'm it."

Damon watched her stand, drawing her book to her chest. "All the light we cannot see," he asked, reading the title. "That's a good one."

When she looked at him a smile escaped her defenses, tugging at the corners of her mouth, but she quickly subdued it. "It won a Pulitzer."

"Naturally. And A well-deserved one."

Tamira made a half turn as if to leave but stopped. As she turned back to Damon, her eyes narrowed. "Are you pranking me or something?"

"Pranking you? No." Damon shook his head. "Why would I be?"

"Forgive me for being suspicious. It wouldn't be the first time."

"Well, I'm not. I'm just having lunch."

Tamira nodded slowly, allowing her eyes to wash over him again. Her heart moaned. He *was* beautiful. "Well then - Damon Kennedy, was it? -the absence of a tray or any food at all lends suspicion to your story." She turned and walked away.

Damon laughed. "Maybe I eat fast," he called after her. Tamira continued walking without a reply. He shook his head and sighed, watching her leave. When she threw him a glance over her shoulder, he smiled. If she'd walked away without looking back, he'd consider himself dead in the water. The look back wasn't much, but it was a crack in her defenses.

He at least had a chance.

"Hi there."

Tamira watched Damon as he joined her, matching her slow pace along the sidewalk. "Wow. Three times in one day. This is getting downright scandalous."

"What?" Damon asked, pulling his backpack over one shoulder.

"Never mind."

"Do you not like me for some reason?" he asked.

"I don't know you, so I neither dislike nor like you." She ducked beneath the corner of a road sign hanging over the sidewalk.

"Well, that's something. I guess."

She stopped and turned to face him; binders clutched to her chest. "Why do you keep seeking me out? You got a bet going or something going on?"

"A bet?"

"Yeah, you know the storyline. The new kid makes a bet he can bring the weird girl out of her shell and make her popular. That kind of thing."

"I don't even have a clue what you're talking about." Damon laughed, shaking his head. "Not even a little bit."

"Don't get to the movies much?" she asked.

"As much as anybody, I guess."

"Perhaps you spend all your free time reading Pulitzer Prize-winning novelists," she said with a sarcastic grin.

Damon laughed. "Okay, I gotta be honest. I just read the title. I haven't read the book. I never even heard of it."

"I am truly shocked." Tamira, smiled, shaking her head.

"Wow. That was kinda harsh." He looked at her profile, examining her gentle features and flawless complexion. She had an elegance about her that most girls their age lacked. He decided that she was pretty, smart, and classy, if somewhat defensive and standoffish.

"Look, did I do something wrong to you?"

"Not yet." She leaned to her right, avoiding a low-hanging branch.

"What does that mean?"

"Nothing." She closed her eyes as she shook her head. "I'm sorry for being rude." They walked in silence until Tamira looked at him again. "I usually try to let most of the others leave to avoid the chaos after school. You must have hung around after the last bell. Why did you do that?"

"I don't know." Damon shrugged, pushing his hands deeper into his pockets. "I just wanted to talk to you. Is that such a bad thing?"

Tamira's eyes searched his face again and she shook her head. "I don't mind, but you'll probably damage your reputation."

Damon laughed. "I'm new here. I don't have a reputation yet. Besides, I think I'll survive."

"I don't know. High school is tough. This one is anyway. Believe me, I know."

"I'll take my chances." Damon matched her pace as she started walking again. "Can I ask you something?"

She spared him a glance before stepping over a cracked piece of sidewalk with an unusual deliberateness. "You can ask. It doesn't mean I'll answer."

"Uh-" Damon cleared his throat. "-will you marry me?"

Tamira stopped suddenly. A length of her hair swung around her neck and landed softly on her shoulder as her head whipped around to face him. Her brow was slightly furrowed above wide green eyes that shone in the afternoon sun as she stared at him, shocked.

"What?"

Damon laughed. "Okay, now that I've asked the most awkward question ever, maybe you'll loosen up."

Her incredulous smile grew into a laugh. "Wow. And people say that I'm weird." She shook her head and started walking again.

Damon walked alongside her while the laughter died. "You seem very skittish. Why is that?" He watched her shoulders draw in as she shrank. She didn't like talking about herself.

"You ask a lot of questions, Damon Kennedy."

He shrugged. "How else do you get to know people?"

"Maybe you could print out a questionnaire. I could fill it out and get it back to you in the morning."

"Ouch. That was harsh, again."

She glanced at him and sighed. "Sorry. I'm not skittish. I'm careful. There's a difference. The world can be a dangerous place. Or haven't you noticed?"

Damon shrugged. "I can't argue with that." He thumbed the strap of his backpack up on his shoulder.

Tamira surveyed the sidewalk in front of them, making sure it was clear, then looked at him. Her eyes darted around his face for a moment, then she dropped her gaze back to the sidewalk.

"It's complicated."

Damon sighed. "I get it. You don't know me. None of my business and all that. I get that."

Tamira stopped again, nodding at a two-story Tudor-style home behind Damon. "This is me."

Damon surveyed the house and nodded. "Nice place."

"It keeps the rain off our heads." Tamira pushed her hair behind her ear and toed a crack in the sidewalk. A strange nervousness began rising in her chest with each second that passed. The sense that she didn't want him to go began to form in her stomach.

"So, uh." Damon ran a hand over his hair and rubbed the back of his neck. "Maybe I could text you or something. I mean if that's okay."

"I don't have a cell phone."

"What?" he asked, shocked. The rumors were true.

Tamira shrugged, shrinking in on herself more. "Who am I going to call? Remember, I'm the weird girl with no friends."

"I don't know." Damon shrugged. "Uh, it's cool though. I guess lots of kids down here don't have them."

She spared him a glance then looked back at her feet. "No. As far as I can tell I'm the only one."

"It's no big deal. Really. I just got mine this past summer."

A soft laugh escaped her. "Uh-huh. I'm sure."

"No. Really. I don't even know how to use all the functions yet."

Tamira looked up at Damon and smiled. "Look, you seem nice. You really do. Why you're being nice to me, I still don't know. But…" she trailed off shaking her head. "I have to go."

Damon watched her mount the three steps to her yard and start down the sidewalk. With her arms clutched in front of her and her head bowed, she looked small again. He shook his head and sighed.

"Hey," he called out to her. Tamira stopped short of her front door but didn't turn around. "Can I walk with you tomorrow?"

Tamira opened the bright red front door to her house and stepped inside. She closed it behind her without looking back.

Damon threw his hands in the air and let them drop to his sides. He stared at the door, waiting for her to open it again and give him an answer. When it didn't happen, he turned and crossed the street, heading in the direction they'd just come.

Chapter Two

"Who was that?"

Tamira peered into the sitting room adjacent to the foyer. The lights were off, and the curtains were drawn, as usual. The scraps of light that snuck past the drapes lay on the floor like ribbons of broken glass.

All the excitement brought on by Damon Kennedy fled her body and she sighed heavily, her shoulders drooping. Today she didn't want to deal with the shadows. She wanted the bright sunlight on her face, and to smile. She'd met a nice boy, and although she didn't expect anything to come of it, she wanted to enjoy the moment.

"Uh, just some guy from school," she said and started up the stairs.

"Tamira," her mother called, the tone of her voice stopping Tamira in her tracks. "Come here please."

Tamira closed her eyes and shook her head. Her smile vanished as she dismounted the few steps she'd claimed and walked into the sitting room.

"How was school?"

"It was fine. Nothing happened."

"Good. Now, who was that?" She held up a hand. "And before you say it, I can see it was a boy, Tamira."

"Mama, he was just some kid from school. He happened to be walking home the same way as me and he was asking about some Algebra problems." Tamira watched her mother nod her head slowly, waiting to see if she was going to press the issue. The look on her face told her that she would.

"Is that all it was?" Crystal Brannigan asked. She'd seen him cross the street and head back in the direction they'd come. This wasn't his way home.

"Yes, Mama. Just some random boy. I don't even know his name."

"Good," she sighed. "Tamira, sweetie, you know I'm just looking out for you. For us."

"I know, Mama," Tamira replied obediently. The resentment in her voice was more prevalent than she intended. She looked up as the sound of her mother rising from her chair filled the quiet room.

"Tamira, we're not like the rest of them. You know that."

"I know Mama, but-"

"There is no but, Tamira." She stepped toward her daughter. A sliver of sunlight fell on her face, and the walls exploded with dozens of tiny multicolored reflections.

Tamira squinted as she followed the light back to her mother's face. Light struck the angles of the fracture on her cheek and refracted in every direction, glittering like diamonds. Her mother always used the wound as an example of how dangerous the world could be for people like them.

"Mama…"

"I know what you're going to say, Tamira." She moved out of the light, plunging the room back into shadows.

"How do you know? Things are different. I'm different."

"Maybe in some ways, but not the ways that matter, sweetie. You know that."

"I'm sick of hiding with you, Mama. I love you, but I'm so tired of being stuck in this house."

"Tamira, I know you understand. It's just a difficult time for you. You're growing into a woman. Things are changing."

"Mama," she protested.

"Just remember, once you're broken Tamira, you can't be fixed. Pop Pop is gone. He can't mend us."

"Mama, I just-" Tamira turned away, not wanting her mother to see her wipe the tear from her cheek. She wanted to turn around and scream into her mother's face, but she didn't dare. She wanted to tell her that their house felt like a prison, that there was a loneliness in her soul that ached. She wanted to say that she hated the dim light and drawn curtains.

She wanted to say a lot of things, but she said nothing.

Crystal Brannigan stared at her daughter, her own heart aching. She knew Tamira craved a life outside these walls, but it was something they couldn't afford. The dangers far outweighed any possible rewards.

She closed her eyes as fingertips went to her cheek, absently dancing over the fracture. She'd been lucky. It could have been much worse.

"How about if we order a pizza?" she asked, masking the ache in her chest. "You like pizza. It'll be fun."

Tamira nodded as she crossed the room to leave. She stopped when her mother called but didn't turn around.

"I'm sorry."

"It's okay, Mama. It's not your fault I'm a freak." Tamira ran from the room before her mother could reply.

Crystal closed her eyes and sighed, dragging the hair from her face. "Nobody said it was going to be easy."

Tamira peeped out her front door and surveyed the sidewalk. To the left, it was clear to the corner. To the right, it was clear to the wall of hedges that separated their yard from the neighbors'. Damon was nowhere in sight. A wry smile slipped across her lips.

She'd had the night to sleep on it and in the end, her mother's cautions had won out. She was making more out of this thing than there was anyway. Damon had walked her home from school, but it didn't mean anything. It was just too dangerous anyway.

She clutched her books to her chest and stepped out the door. Looking around again, a part of her admitted that it wouldn't have been the worst thing if the boy named Damon Kennedy were here. It would be nice to have a boy walk her to school.

But he isn't here, her mind told her. "It's for the best anyway," she told herself as she started walking. Sure, he had a wild crop of wavy hair that she wanted to run her hands through, and brown, soulful eyes that she wanted to get lost in, but it was probably for the best that he wasn't here. He was nice, and he was cute and had a nice smile, but that was it. Well, he also had a little adventurous air to him that might have been fun, if not a little dangerous.

A knot formed in her stomach and her lips slid into a half-smile as she made her way down the sidewalk. He had sought her out three times yesterday, but why? He didn't seem the type to let his friends put him up to be mean. There was a genuineness to him, a comforting demeanor that made her want to trust him.

It doesn't matter now anyway, she thought. He was just being nice. That's all it was. He's new. His friends will change his mind soon enough and he'll join the ranks of everybody else. Within a few days, he'll be solidly in the cool crowd, and you'll still be the weird girl, and he won't even look at you. At least this way, my mother would be happy.

She took the three steps down to the sidewalk slowly, being careful not to catch her heel on the edge. A fall here would be devastating. Turning right, she headed to school. It was for the best, she told herself again, but the voice in her head sounded more like her mother's than her own.

"Good morning." As Tamira drew even with the shrubs, Damon stood from the low stone wall that lined her neighbor's yard.

She gasped, recoiling quickly. Her hands flew up defensively. A yelp escaped her when she felt her feet become entangled. Her books went flying and she pinwheeled her arms to regain her balance, but it was too late. She was falling! She closed her eyes as the sound of her scream filled the air. No, she thought. This can't be happening. I can't be falling. No.

In an instant, a thousand warnings from her mother sounded in her mind like alarm bells. You could break. You can never be repaired. You're too young to be broken. Don't take chances. You're risking everything. You could break. You could shatter!

The image of her shattering filled her mind. All her life it had been the one thing she feared the most. Like her mother, she could survive a break, but if she shattered…

Tamira drew herself tight and closed her eyes, anticipating the pain of hitting the concrete. She would break, but she could save her face. She didn't want to be like her mother.

My arm, she thought. My left arm. I'll put my left arm out to catch myself. I'm right-handed, so I could live without my left. Things will be harder, but I can learn to manage.

If her arm broke, her mother would make her stop going to school, but that would be okay. She wouldn't be completely broken. She'd survive at least. She wouldn't shatter.

"Are you okay?"

Tamira's breath caught in her throat as she slowly became aware that she was no longer falling. Something had stopped her. Someone had caught her. Someone who smelled like warm chocolate and had two strong arms was holding her tight.

She opened her eyes and found Damon's wide-eyed stare looking down at her. For an instant, her fear disappeared, and she absorbed the moment. His face was inches from hers. His eyes were locked on hers. His arms were around her.

"Are you okay?" Damon asked again, bent over her as if he were dipping her in a dance scene from the movies. He'd closed the distance between them and caught her before she'd fallen far at all.

"Yes," she squeaked, her breath barely escaping her throat. She could feel his heart beating in his hand against her back. The faint, sweet smell of chocolate surrounded her again. Despite her fear, a slight smile escaped her lips.

"I didn't mean to scare you. I was just sitting here scrolling through my phone, and then there you were." He put her back on her feet and stepped back. "I thought I'd say something to keep from scaring you, but I guess that's what scared you. I'm sorry."

Tamira nodded absently. "Uh-huh," she said, wondering what had just happened. She shook her head. She looked down at herself to make sure nothing had broken, then at Damon. He was staring at her with a look that was both shocked and bemused.

"Are you sure you're okay?" Damon looked at her, unsure what to do next. She was breathing heavy, and her cheeks were red as fire. There was a sleepy, confused look in her eyes.

"I'm fine," she said, nodding her head as her eyes darted around his face. "I'm okay. You're…"

"Damon Kennedy."

"Yes," she whispered, still nodding. "Damon Kennedy. I-I'm okay."

Damon nodded with her as a smile broke out on his face. Her voice sounded more like she was reassuring herself than him. "Are you sure, because you still seem pretty shook?"

Tamira knew she was swooning but couldn't help it. She'd just been in his arms, his lips inches from hers. His gorgeous eyes were locked on hers. His arms were around her. God, he smelled so good.

"Tamira?"

Her eyes flew open as reality came crashing in around her. She gasped and looked over her shoulder. She couldn't see her house from here. With any luck, the shrubs had blocked her mother's view from the window. Maybe she hadn't seen.

"Uh. I'm fine," Tamira lied. Her heart pounded against her chest and her knees suddenly felt weak. She staggered to the wall and sat down, taking a deep breath to gather herself.

She'd almost fallen, potentially shattering. There was also the possibility that her mother had seen it. That in and of itself would open a whole new set of problems. But despite all that, her mind kept returning to the fact that Damon had sat and waited for her so they could walk together.

"I'm sorry," Damon said with an innocent laugh.

"It's not funny," Tamira snapped. "I could have been seriously hurt." She didn't tell him how seriously. The truth was that a fall like that could have easily broken her irreparably, maybe even killed her.

Tamira rubbed her forehead, trying to sort the storm of emotions running through her mind. She shook her head and looked up at the boy who had both nearly killed and saved her.

Now what do I do, she wondered?

Standing in the front room window, clutching the heavy drape in her hand, Crystal Brannigan sighed and shook her head. She'd caught only a glimpse of her daughter's near catastrophe, but it was enough to stop her heart for a moment. She couldn't see who had caught her, avoiding disaster, but she had a good idea who it was. It was probably the same boy who had walked her home yesterday.

As Tamira, and whoever she was talking to, moved beyond the shrubbery, she released the curtain and turned from the window. She was beyond her sight now and on her own.

Crystal drew in another deep breath shook her head again. Tamira was growing up and her ability to protect her was waning. If only she could make her realize the risk that she took every day by refusing to be homeschooled. Opting instead to go out into a harsh world full of hard edges, any one of which could fracture her flawless complexion.

Or she could fall, Crystal thought as a shudder ran through her. Her hand went to the two-inch fissure on her left cheek. She was broken and beyond repair, but she'd do whatever it took to keep the same thing from happening to her precious daughter.

"I know it's not funny," Damon said, erasing his smile. "I'm sorry, really." He looked at her, nodding. Some of the flush was leaving her cheeks. They were still a rosy pink, but only enough to make her eyes stand out. They were intense and alive, and he decided that they were beautiful.

Tamira put a hand to her chest and took another deep breath. "I know. It's fine. Just promise me you'll never do that again?"

"Okay. I promise." Damon gathered her books from the sidewalk and brought them to her. "So, if I have to promise to never do that again, does that mean you're going to let me walk you to school?"

Tamira shook her head and started organizing her things. "I can't make you do anything. You can do what you want. The sidewalk is city property. I don't own it."

Tamira scolded herself. What are you doing? Tell him yes. Yes, he can walk you to school every day. He could walk her to school forever if he wanted to.

"Well, I've been thinking about it," Damon shoved his hands in his pockets and nodded. "I think I'd like to keep talking to you. And walking with you too."

Tamira was able to hide her smile, but the flush returned to her cheeks. She could feel the heat rise in them but couldn't stop it. He'd been thinking about her. This gorgeous guy was thinking about her. Her? And he wanted to keep walking her to school.

"I have to tell you something," she said standing. She took a deep breath to gather herself and released it slowly. She looked him in the eye and cocked one brow. "For the record, I think you're pranking me."

"Why would I prank you?"

"Because your jerky friends put you up to it, that's why."

"I'm not pranking you. Geesh. Give a guy a break already."

Tamira shook her head. "Uh-huh. That is exactly what someone trying to prank me would say."

"It's exactly what someone *not* trying to prank you would say too because it would be true. You ever consider that?"

She stared at him as he stood in the dappled light filtering through an old-growth oak tree in her neighbor's yard. His eyes were vibrant, and his smile assailed her defenses. "Touché, Damon Kennedy."

Tamira shrugged, tossing her hair back over her shoulder. She sighed and shook her head. "It's probably a bad idea, but after careful deliberation, I've decided to let you walk with me."

"Good. That's better."

"But only because I saw some bees around the other day. You might be useful to kill them." She looked at him and a smile slipped across her lips. "Or maybe as a distraction while I get away."

Damon nodded, falling in beside her as she started walking. "So, if we see a beehive, I'm supposed to throw myself on top of it, so you won't get stung?"

"Generally, yes."

"Don't you care if I get stung?"

She sighed. "To be perfectly honest, you deserve to get stung for leaping out of the bushes like the Boston Strangler and scaring people half to death."

"I've already apologized for scaring you. And I was just sitting there. I hardly think that qualifies as 'leaping out of the bushes'."

"Just the same, you're lucky. This time."

Damon watched her run a hand along the length of her hair. She swept it around her neck and over her far shoulder. His eyes washed over the graceful lines of her neck, and he smiled. Her jawline was smooth and delicate, her skin free of the freckles common to many natural redheads.

Walking with her chin up, she looked strong and independent. Her gentle features and slender neck gave her an air of sophistication, like a princess.

He put a hand to his chest as a stirring began within it. There was something about her that beckoned to him. He'd felt it the first time he saw her, and the feeling had only grown. He couldn't pinpoint what it was, but there was something.

He tugged on his backpack strap as they walked. "So, anyway. Why would you think I was pranking you?"

Tamira looked at him. She shook her head, smiling. Because, her mind told her, that would be the only reason a guy like this would pursue her. "Let's just say this-" she wagged her finger between them, "-doesn't happen very often. Or ever, really."

"Well, believe it or not, I'm not pranking you. Nobody put me up to anything. I just thought it would be nice to walk with you, to maybe get to know you more."

"Why?" she asked, giving him a fleeting glance.

"Why walk with you?" He shrugged. "I don't know. Because if we ran to school, we'd get all sweaty."

Tamira laughed harder than she meant to. "You're goofy."

"Thanks," he laughed. "That's what I was going for. Some guys try to be all suave and cool, but not me. I go straight for goofy."

"How's that working out for you?"

Damon looked at her, one eyebrow cocked slightly. "So far, so good."

Tamira felt a fire ignite in her face again as her heart swelled in her chest. It was suddenly hard to breathe. She turned away, hoping to hide her reaction.

"Are you okay?" he asked.

"Um-hum," she said nodding, still unable to look at him. "I'm good."

Damon smiled. He'd taken a chance openly flirting with her, but her reaction told him it had paid off. He'd broken the ice. Hopefully, she'd see that he wasn't like the other guys.

"So, did you think I was going to spend weeks being nice to you just so I could invite you to some dance so my friends could pour cow blood on you or something?"

"Uh, no," she said with an incredulous laugh. "Where would you even get that idea?"

"It was in a movie or something. I think."

"That's just horrible. Who would do that?"

Damon shrugged. "I don't know. Not me. If it's any consolation, it didn't work out well for them. I think she killed everybody."

"Wow. Sounds like a really interesting family movie night."

He shrugged. "Well, anyway, the point is that I'm not playing a joke on you."

"You better not be."

"I'm not."

"Because, if you are, you should know something." She narrowed her eyes as she looked at him. "I know people."

Damon laughed. "Really? *You* know people?"

"What?" she asked with a grin, lifting her chin into the air indignantly. "I can know people. You don't know who I know."

"True. True. It's just that most people with underworld connections aren't cute redheads."

Tamira's breath caught in her throat, and she coughed to disguise it. Did he say cute, she asked herself? He did. He said she was cute. She looked at him and shrugged. "Well," was all she could squeeze out.

Damon shrugged, still smiling. "I guess I better straighten up and fly right then."

Tamira nodded her head and smiled at him. "That's right. I'm watching you, Damon Kennedy." She pointed two fingers at her own eyes, then stabbed them toward his.

"Good," he said with a smirk. "Because I'll be watching you too."

Tamira felt her legs begin to quiver, sure that she must be dreaming. Any minute now her alarm would sound, and she'd wake up. She drew in a deep breath to calm her nerves. Please, she thought, if I'm dreaming let me have five more minutes.

Chapter Three

Damon waved to Tamira as she approached him on the sidewalk in front of the school. "It's me. Here, out in the open, being the least surprising that a person can be."

Tamira's lips tried to smile, but she wouldn't let them. She paused in front of Damon, unable to look at him, then continued walking without speaking.

"Hey," Damon said, catching up with her. "Is something wrong?"

"No. I don't guess there is."

"What's up? I didn't see you at lunch."

"I had some work to do in the library." Tamira kept her eyes forward as she walked. She wanted desperately to look at him but knew that her resolve would vanish if she did. She wanted to stare into his brown eyes and watch his smile gently curve his lips, but she didn't. She'd had all day to think about her near fall and the enormity of the situation weighed heavily on her. Had she fallen and hit the sidewalk any number of things could have happened. None of which were good.

"Okay." Damon shrugged. "Are you alright? You seem angry. Did something happen? Was it Brady and those jerks again?"

"Nothing happened."

"Then what's up?"

Tamira looked around, then lead him to the edge of the sidewalk and away from traffic. "Nothing's up. Nobody did anything that they don't usually do."

"If they did, I could tell them to lay off you."

"I don't need you to protect me, Damon Kennedy," she snapped.

"Okay," he said, holding his hands out in front of him. "I'm sorry."

Tamira shook her head and sighed. "Don't apologize."

"Okay, I'm sorry. I mean, I won't." Her demeanor had changed drastically since the morning. Something was bothering her.

"Look, you're a super nice guy. I believe that. I really do, but this might all be too much."

"What this? I'm just talking to you."

"And walking me home, and to school this morning."

"So that's a bad thing now? I thought you kinda liked it this morning."

"That's not it." She sighed, looking skyward. "I just can't," she said, shaking her head. "It's just…no. I'm sorry."

Damon shook his head, hurt by her rejection. "Okay, fine. I can take a hint. Dang. I mean, how dare I be nice? I just wanted to walk with you. I thought maybe we could be friends or something." Damon back-peddled a few steps, shaking his head. "You know, I'm new here. You're not the only one with problems, Tamira. But hey, I won't bother you again." He threw a dismissive wave in her direction and walked away.

Tamira's breath caught in her throat and her chest swelled with a deep ache. Tears welled in her eyes. She didn't want him to go, but how could she continue to let things move forward? It would never work out. It would be better if it all stopped before it got started. He was nice and cute, and there was just something about him that she wanted to be near, but he was too dangerous for her. Things would be better if she let him walk away.

Her mother was right. Just going to school was crazy. What was wrong with her? Did she have a suicide wish?

"Wait." Tamira's voice was a surprise to her own ears. Why did she stop him? It didn't make any sense. She knew she should let him go, but she didn't want to.

Damon stopped and turned back to her. He shrugged his backpack up on his left shoulder and threw a hand up at her. "What?"

Tamira walked back to him and jerked her head in the direction they'd been walking. "We're just walking, okay?"

"I never said it was anything but that."

Tamira groaned quietly. This was a bad idea. It would end badly. It was silly. It was a bad idea, but it felt good. She'd never felt like this before, and she didn't want it to stop.

"Well," she began, giving in to what she wanted instead of what she knew she should do. A sly grin came to her lips as she looked at him. "Technically, you did propose to me. That's more than just walking."

Damon laughed. "I was kidding. You know that, right?"

"Um-hum," she answered. "Sure it was. That's what they all say."

"Oh, so a lot of boys have proposed to you?"

"Well, I mean, you're the first to actually come out and say it."

Damon nodded. "I see." He looked at Tamira. She was smiling. It was a beautiful smile. "I'm glad you stopped me back there."

"I'm glad you didn't keep walking. I'm sorry I was rude."

"To be honest, I was walking as slow as I could to give you a chance to change your mind."

Tamira laughed. "Were you now?"

Damon nodded, laughing himself. "I was."

"What would you have done if I didn't call you back?"

Damon shrugged. "Maybe some big, goofy gesture that you couldn't ignore."

"Hmm. That sounds interesting. Like what?" She gathered her hair and pulled it over her shoulder, playing with the end absently.

"I don't know. Maybe skywriting or something."

"Can you fly a plane?" she asked giggling.

"No."

"That might complicate things for you."

"I didn't say it was a good plan."

Tamira stepped closer to him, bumping him with her shoulder as she gave a wide berth to the back of a mailbox.

"You okay there?" Damon asked.

"I'm good," she answered with a nod. "Just didn't wanna run into that mailbox."

Damon's eyes narrowed. "You're very careful, aren't you?"

"Is there anything wrong with that?" she asked, sparing him a glance.

"No," he began. "Not exactly, but I've noticed that you're extremely careful not to touch stuff." He shrugged. "It's just an observation."

"Isn't everybody careful to some extent?" she asked, already knowing the answer. "Aren't you?"

Damon chuckled. "I don't guess. I mean, it's not like I go around throwing myself into walls or juggling sticks of dynamite or anything.

"Careful is a good thing. Besides, you can't even buy dynamite without a permit so…"

"You've checked?"

Tamira shrugged. "You don't know me. I might have."

Damon shrugged. "Do you have a germ phobia?"

"Wow. That came out of left field." Tamira laughed as she made an exaggerated step to clear a broken piece of concrete on the sidewalk. "Is that what your friends told you?"

Damon shrugged. "Maybe."

"The answer is no. I don't have a germ phobia. However, I've never been sick, so there's that."

"You've never been sick? Not even a cold?"

"Nope," she said shaking her head. "Neither has my mom."

"Well, I guess whatever you're doing is paying off."

"Yes," she said, giving him a matter-of-fact look. "Like I said, careful is a good thing."

"Don't you think there's such thing as being too careful?"

"Nope."

"Not even a little bit?" he asked.

"No."

"Okay," he said, dragging the word out as he shook his head. "You know. Sometimes a little risk can be fun."

"Trust me, I know," Tamira laughed. "You have no idea how much I know that."

"You don't seem like a risk taker, Tamira. Not even a little bit."

"I'm no stunt pilot, but there are lots of things you don't know about me."

Damon smiled. "Maybe you'll hang out with me long enough to let me know some of them."

She stopped and looked at him. "You can be quite forward sometimes, can't you?"

"Is that a bad thing?"

"No. Just an observation." She smiled and started walking again, bending down to avoid the same traffic sign as yesterday.

"See," Damon said, rejoining her. "Like that. Most people just sidestep or bend their head, but you go way out of your way to avoid bumping into stuff."

"So?" she asked. "Should I just walk into stuff like some kind of idiot?"

"No," Damon replied with a grin. "Unless you're training to be a stunt double." He watched her smile out of the corner of his eye. "You have a wonderful smile, you know."

"Oh, stop," she replied, covering her face with her hand.

"Seriously. You do."

"Thank you." Tamira felt herself blush again.

"So, uh, back there, why didn't you want me to walk with you?"

Tamira's smile vanished. "I never said I didn't want you to walk with me."

"That's sure what it sounded like to me."

"I said it wasn't a good idea."

"Isn't that the same thing?" he asked.

"No. Not even close." Tamira shook her head.

"Okay." Damon shrugged his backpack up on his shoulder as he stared at her. "You do want me to walk with you, but you think it's a bad idea?"

"More or less, yes." She sighed. "It's complicated."

Tamira stopped and turned to him, clutching her books to her chest. "Well, Damon Kennedy, you've successfully walked me home, again."

Damon looked at the house and nodded. "Yup. I'm getting good at this." He pulled at the strap of his backpack and sighed. "So, you said you don't have a cell. Do you have a landline?"

"Like a regular phone?"

Damon nodded, smiling. "Yeah, like a regular phone."

"Of course. We're not cavemen."

"You don't have a cellphone," Damon mumbled with a laugh.

"What was that?" she asked nudging him playfully.

"I said, uh, it's a good thing all the wells are gone?"

"The wells are gone. Really? I don't think that's what you said."

"Yeah, you know, like in the old days. Kids were always falling in wells and stuff. It's a good thing they're gone."

Tamira laughed. "You're full of it. You know that, right? It was a good recovery, but I'm not buying it."

Damon laughed with her. "What? It was horrible. Kids stuck in wells and stuff, having to send dogs for help. It was a tragic time in our history as a nation really." He nodded. "Dark days."

Tamira shook her head, still laughing as she mounted the steps.

"So, can I maybe call you sometimes?" he called as she walked down the sidewalk to her front door.

Tamira looked over her shoulder at him. "I guess that'd be okay." She threw him a wave. "Bye now."

"What's your number?" Damon watched the door close and shook his head. He threw his hands in the air and let them drop with an exasperated groan. "I don't have your number."

Tamira fell back against the inside of the door with a long sigh, squeezing her books to her chest as a smile broke out on her lips. She knew she shouldn't let herself like this guy so much, but she couldn't help it. Damon was the first boy to pay her this much attention and he was cute and funny, and amazing.

Even though he'd just caught her to prevent a fall, the feeling of his arms around her was the best thing she'd ever felt, and she was counting it as a hug. It was something she'd like to experience again.

"Tamira."

The sound of her mother's voice shattered her enthusiasm. The smile slipped from Tamira's face, and her shoulders fell.

"Yes, Mama."

"Can you come in here for a minute?" There was a brief pause then she added, "Please."

Tamira deposited her books on the bottom of the staircase and plodded into the sitting room.

"Come here, sweetie."

Tamira walked into her mother's open arms.

"You know how much I love you, don't you?"

"I know, Mama. I love you too," she replied obediently.

"I know you do." Crystal stroked her daughter's hair. "You know what I want to talk about, don't you?"

Tamira nodded against her mother's chest.

"Sweetie, I worry for you so much. There are dangers everywhere."

"I'm okay, Mama. I'm very careful," Tamira said.

"Are you?" Crystal kissed the top of her daughter's head then rested her chin on it. "Were you very careful this morning?"

Tamira's heart stopped. She had seen! "But mama, it was nothing. It probably looked worse from the window."

"Yes, I know sweetie. Everything looks worse from the window. You've said it before, but I know what I saw."

"Nothing happened."

"You almost fell."

"But I didn't, Mama. I didn't fall."

"You did fall."

"I didn't fall all the way to the ground," Tamira replied defiantly. It was splitting hairs and she knew it, but she had to say something.

Crystal nodded. "I know. He caught you, didn't he?"

"Yes," Tamira said, fighting back tears.

"But he also made you fall, didn't he?"

"He didn't mean to. I just wasn't expecting him to be there. It was my fault."

Crystal pushed her daughter off her chest and held her at arm's length. She shook her head and looked into her eyes, drawing in a deep breath to calm her worries.

Tamira looked up at her mother. A strip of light from the window fell across her face, touching off her piercing blue eyes. When the light hit them like this, they were almost translucent, like ice.

"It wasn't your fault, Tamira and you know it. Don't make excuses."

"It's not like that, Mama. It was an innocent mistake. I told him not to do it anymore and he said he wouldn't."

Crystal pulled her daughter back to her chest and embraced her. "If only things were that simple, sweetie." She sighed and said it again. "If only things were so simple."

Damon watched his video game character, a paramilitary commando, creep along a battered brick wall, his massive gun at the ready. He had spent the last two hours scouring the ruined city to find his friends and kill them.

His character dropped suddenly to his knees as blood poured from his head. You have been killed by: PUNISHER364 appeared on the screen above his character.

"What? How?"

Brady's laugh came over the headset. "Gotcha."

"Oh my god, what a sweet shot," Easton added, laughing.

"Where were you?" Damon asked. "I never saw you."

"That's the whole point of a sniper, genius," Brady replied.

"Well, crap. Guess I'm done," Damon said. "Later guys."

"Wait, aren't you gonna hang out and watch?" Easton asked. "I still got three more people to kill."

"Yeah, man. C'mon. What else you got to do?" Brady added.

Damon sighed and shook his head. "My dad's been on me to do some chores around here. I just need to get them done." A chorus of "Lame" came through his headset.

"He probably wants to go hang out with Tamira Brannigan," Easton teased.

"Really, guys? C'mon." Damon said.

"Look, man. I know you've been secretly talking to her. What's up with that?"

"Yeah, what's up with that?" Brady echoed.

"First of all, I haven't been doing anything in secret. We've talked in public, and walked in public, some. It's no big deal." Damon shook his head. "Besides, why do you guys care anyway. You'll always have each other."

"Very funny." Easton pressed him on the issue. "Seriously, she's so weird. Are you guys going to get married or something?"

"Dude, you're an idiot. You know that, right?"

"For real though. What's going on?" Brady asked.

"So. I've talked to her. She doesn't have the plague. She's nice. Besides, it's none of your business anyway," Damon snapped.

"She's some kinda weirdo, man. People are already talking about you. I had to defend you in Math class yesterday."

Damon sighed. "I don't need you or anybody to defend me. Who's talking about me?"

"I'd rather not say right now," Easton replied. "But it just goes to show you what damage could be done hanging out with this weirdo."

"She's not a weirdo!" Damon's voice was sharper than he intended. He closed his eyes and shook his head, listening to the silence on his headset. "I mean, c'mon man, she's just a regular person. Leave people alone."

"Yeah. Okay, man. Whatever," Easton finally said.

"Yeah, man. Whatever."

Damon rubbed his face with both hands, then slid the headset off. He cued the mic and said, "I gotta go, guys. My dad is calling me." He dropped it to the table and switched off the game console.

He spun in his chair and stood, going to his bed. He picked up his phone and checked it for messages. Though he knew it was impossible, he briefly hoped that there would be one from Tamira.

Damon stared at his reflection on the phone screen. Watching his hand rub his chin, he let out a long sigh. He could probably find Tamira's number. It wouldn't be that difficult. A simple reverse search. He had her name and address. Easy Peasy.

But then what? he wondered. If you called her, she'd wonder how you got her number. Then she'd think you were a stalker. Or maybe she knows how easy it is and is testing to see if you're an idiot who can't even do a reverse search online, his mind suggested.

Damon shook his head and tossed the phone onto his bed. No, he was going to err on the side of caution. Tamira was different. She wasn't weird, but she was unique. Looking up her phone number and calling her out of the blue would probably freak her out.

He dropped onto the bed, laying back with a moan as he tried to figure out his feelings for Tamira. She was interesting and different. Those were good things. She was also smart and funny. Kinda sassy too, he thought with a smile. And she's pretty. She was everything, except popular.

Damon pursed his lips as he saw Tamira in his mind. She was tall for a girl, and a little gangly, which probably went with the territory of being tall. Her dark red hair was nice, but she didn't do much with it. She had green eyes that sparkled in the right light. That was nice. Her eyebrows were perfectly shaped arches that framed her eyes well. She was thin, but he'd noticed a few nice curves. And she has a pretty neck, he thought, laughing at himself.

She has a nice smile too, he thought, a smile coming to his own lips. And thin, cute lips. He wondered what it would be like to kiss her and decided it would probably be amazing.

The idea of her quirky behavior burst into his mind, and his smile faded. Okay, he thought, maybe she's not the most popular girl in school. She also wasn't an uptight, pretentious snob. Standoffish, maybe, but approachable if a guy was willing to put in the time.

She did make an extreme effort to keep from running into things. Was that so weird? Damon grabbed his phone and went to the internet. Maybe Tamira had some sort of syndrome or something. That might explain things.

After half an hour slogging through various psychoses, he stumbled across a medical condition that explained everything. "Osteogenesis imperfecta," he said aloud, reading the diagnosis.

It was a condition commonly called Brittle Bone Syndrome. It left the person with bones that broke easily and lead to sensitive skin that could also be easily damaged.

Damon sighed heavily, nodding. It would explain her peculiar behavior and her over cautiousness. Part of him was relieved that there was a "normal" reason for the way she acted, but part of him wondered if he wanted to date a "sick" girl.

He settled back on the bed and began reading about the disease. When Tamira warned him that she was "complicated", she wasn't kidding.

After a few paragraphs, he gave up and dropped his phone. He already had the answer to his question. He didn't need to read more. Interlacing his fingers behind his head, he closed his eyes. The image of Tamira floated into his mind again, and he smiled.

The moment was brief, but his mind replayed it slowly. She turned her head to look at him and her hair swung around, landing on her shoulder, shining in the afternoon sun. The light coming through the trees struck her eyes, highlighting the different shades of green. Her thin smile grew as she looked at him. She blinked once, then looked away, her cheeks blushing slightly.

This girl, he thought, shaking his head as another smile slid across his face.

Chapter Four

Damon strolled along the smooth asphalt surface of the walking trail next to Tamira. They'd fallen into an awkward silence, giving him time to evaluate the past week. They'd walked to and from school every day and had eaten lunch together most of the week. Their conversations had become smooth and effortless. He enjoyed being with her, but not only as a potential girlfriend. She was smart and witty, beautiful, and tough. He genuinely enjoyed being with her.

He was glad that she agreed to meet him at the park, but his mind was struggling with a way to bring up the subject of Tamira's disease. He wanted to tell her it didn't matter. He wanted to know, but just so he'd know what to expect, how he should be with her.

"Are you okay?" she asked quietly, breaking the silence.

"Me? Oh, yeah. I'm good." Damon glanced at her, then looked away rubbing the back of his neck.

"Because you seem like something's bothering you."

Damon shook his head. "No. I don't guess there is."

Tamira opened her mouth to speak but closed it. Her mother hadn't completely bought her excuse of going to the library and had questioned her suspiciously, but in the end, relented. Tamira didn't like lying to her, but there was no way she could resist being with Damon in a non-school-related setting. The high hopes she'd woken up with were circling the drain now, however. Something was wrong.

The forced, sporadic conversation, the long stretches of silence, and the uneasiness with which he held himself telegraphed Damon's discomfort.

Tamira sighed. The corners of her mouth pulled downward. She had an idea what was wrong but didn't want to admit it. Damon was sweet, funny, and gorgeous, and she was the weird girl. That put him out of her league. His friends were probably giving him grief for hanging out with her. They'd had a full week since school started to put pressure on him and he was finally succumbing to it.

He'd asked her to the park to tell her that they couldn't hang out anymore. That way there wouldn't be a scene at school. He'd say something like, "It's not personal. You know how it is at school," and she'd say something like, "It's okay. No big deal."

Then he'd walk away, and she'd find a quiet corner of the park and cry. Of course, she'd put on a brave face at school. She was used to doing that. Every time she saw him, she'd pretend it didn't bother her no matter how her heart ached. She'd act like she didn't want to be with him. Things would go on and time would pass. Eventually, she'd learn to be content with a few days of pleasant memories.

She scolded herself for allowing herself to like him so much so soon. She liked hanging out with him. She liked talking to him and even just looking at him. She liked the way her heart fluttered when they touched, even if it was accidental. She liked the way his wavy hair was a mess by the end of school and the way one corner of his mouth was slightly higher than the other when he smiled. He was funny and witty, and she didn't want him to stop talking to her.

Despite her best efforts to stop them, her feelings for him were becoming very real. She'd moved too fast, even for a 'normal' girl. She should have known better. How could a boy like him ever really care for a girl like her?

But it wasn't her fault. It was his fault for being so damned charming and cute and smelling so good. He'd sought her out, he'd sat with her. And now he was going to break up with her.

Tamira kicked a pinecone from the path, watching it bounce along the grass. It passed close to a squirrel, sending it scurrying across the path in front of them and up a tree. She sighed and looked at Damon. His eyes weren't sparkling like they had been all week, and there was no trace of a smile on his lips.

"The weather's nice." Her voice faltered slightly, but he didn't seem to notice.

"Yeah. Probably get hot later though," he replied quietly.

She pushed a hand through the hair that she'd painstakingly brushed and styled only a few hours ago. Her eyes scanned his face as he stared down at the bike path. There was a sadness there that made her heart ache.

Tamira stopped suddenly, shaking her head. She couldn't take it anymore. They were both miserable. "Let's just get this over with. Okay?"

"Get what over with?"

"This," she said, waving her hand between them. "You have something to say, so just go ahead and say it.

You didn't ask me here to make small talk about the weather. I mean, we're not like forty years old, or something. Who even talks about the weather? It's just a way to fill the awkward silence when two people don't know what to say to each other."

"Okay." His eyes searched her face. "We don't have to talk about the weather."

"Look, I know it's not personal and I know how high school is. If you don't want to hang out with me, it's okay. Just go. It's fine, really. I'm giving you an out. You don't even have to say anything. Just walk away. I just can't take another minute of waiting for the hammer to drop."

Damon's eyes narrowed as he stared at her. Her brow was furrowed over her wet, glossy eyes. Her already thin lips were pursed tightly. "What are you even talking about?" he asked.

She pushed both hands through her hair and interlaced her fingers behind her head. "That's why you're acting so weird, so awkward. You're too nice to come out and say it."

"Say what?"

Tamira sighed, dropping her hands. "That your friends are hassling you about hanging out with the weird girl and that you don't wanna talk to me anymore."

Damon shook his head in wide, slow movements as he stared back at her. "That's not true at all. Well, they have given me a little grief, but I'm not sweating those goofballs. They're idiots." His eyes settled on hers. "And nothing about you is weird."

Tamira looked at him, her eyes darting around his face as she examined his surprise. "Then what is it? What do you want to say? Spit it out, Damon Kennedy."

Damon ran a hand over his hair and looked away with a sigh. "Are you sick?" he asked.

"Sick?" she asked, surprised. "No. I told you that I've never been sick."

Damon looked at her and shrugged. "Not like sick with a cold, but like sick, sick."

"I'm not following you. You're going to have to be more specific. My mind was in a whole 'nother place."

"Do you have osteogenesis imperfecta?"

She stared at him, absorbing the tortured expression on his face. "You think…" A laugh escaped her, and she clasped a hand over her mouth to stop it. She looked at him, shaking her head.

"It's not funny," he said, embarrassed.

"I'm sure it's not. It's a pretty long name. Sounds serious."

"Do you have it?"

"I'm pretty sure I'd know if I had something like that."

Damon sighed, relieved, but still confused. He'd been so sure that he'd found out why she acted the way she did. "It's commonly called Brittle Bone Disease."

A twisted smile slid across her face as they began walking again. "I don't have any kind of disease." She nodded, arranging the situation in her mind. He'd been trying to figure out why she was so careful. It was nice that he'd been thinking about her but concerning that he'd gone to such lengths to figure out why she acted the way she did. That meant it was bothering him.

"So, you think I'm some disease-riddled weirdo?" she asked smiling, nudging him with her shoulder.

"No," Damon insisted, his cheeks flushing red. "I was just trying to figure out why you're so careful." He shrugged. "You have to admit that you do seem overly cautious."

"And you thought if I had brittle bones, it would explain it? There'd be a medical reason that I acted weird and that would make it more acceptable."

"I never said you were weird."

"Whatever." Tamira ran both hands over her hair again. She shook her head, trying to figure out how she felt about his revelation. "I don't have a disease, okay. I'm not sick. I don't have any kind of psychosis or behavioral issues or ticks. I don't have any type of mental disorder either, to save you some research time."

"Okay. Good." Damon tossed his hands into the air. "I'm sorry. I didn't mean to imply anything. I just…"

Tamira stole a glance at him as they walked. As sad as it was, it was probably the most effort any boy had ever put forth for her in her whole life. Okay, she thought, he thinks I'm a little weird, but he's still here. That means something, doesn't it?

"Damon," she said with a sigh. "I know your friends probably do give you grief about hanging out with me."

"I don't care. They're morons." He nodded at her. "I really don't."

"That is true," she said with a laugh. "They are morons. *But,* if hanging out with me makes your life even a little more difficult, you don't owe me an explanation. You can just go. It's okay, really."

51

"What if I don't wanna go?" he asked. "I mean, if you want me to go just tell me to go away and the next thing you'll see will be me going away." He looked at her. "But I don't want to."

"I never said I *wanted* you to."

"Good. I don't want to either," he replied.

"Good."

"Good."

They walked in silence for a few minutes before Damon reached out and took her hand in his. Her body tensed for an instant, then relax. He looked away, hiding the broad smile on his face. Her hand felt good in his.

Tamira gasped internally as Damon's hand found hers. Her heart thundered in her chest. This was big. It was huge, but what did it mean? Were they "together" now? Were they dating?

"So..." Damon began. "It's nice out this morning."

"Yeah," she agreed. Her words didn't want to come out of her throat because her heart was lodged in it. "Probably get hot later though."

Damon carried two hot dogs and two drinks across the grass and sat down on the park bench next to Tamira. He gave her one of each and refused her offer to pay for her meal.

She smiled at him and tucked a stray lock of hair behind her ear. "Thank you."

"No problem," he said casually, before digging into his lunch.

Tamira nibbled at her food despite being hungry. She didn't want to seem like an ogre. In the lunchroom at school, the pretty girls always just picked at their meal. They spent most of their lunch break socializing and laughing at their boyfriend's lame jokes.

She liked this boy. He'd held her hand until their palms were sweaty, so she assumed he liked her too. Inside, she was screaming with joy and doing a happy dance, but the small, dark voice of worry that sounded a lot like her mother, kept chiming in.

She was different. There was no way around it. She avoided people at school, and thus had no friends. Until Damon, no boy had ever paid her very much attention, so she'd never had a boyfriend. Until now it had been easy to hide. Now she couldn't hide anymore. Now she had a reason not to.

Damon spared Tamira a glance as he finished the last of his hot dog. She'd barely eaten anything and was now staring off into space, lost in thought. When she sighed heavily, he asked her what was wrong.

"Oh, nothing," she lied. Everything was wrong, but everything was also very right at the same time. She never thought she'd be in this situation. She wasn't prepared for this.

"You sure? That sigh sounded like something was wrong."

Tamira smiled at him, then dropped her gaze to the hot dog in her hands. "Why do you like me?"

Damon wadded the hot dog wrapper and tossed it into the trashcan next to the bench, buying himself some time to come up with an answer. When he turned back to Tamira, he still didn't have one.

"I don't know. At first, I just thought you were pretty."

Tamira blushed. "Stop."

"Seriously. I thought you were cute. Maybe I like redheads. I don't know."

She smiled, struggling to contain her excitement. "Well, thank you."

"Really? You don't see it do you?"

"See what?"

"That you're beautiful?"

Tamira shook her head and looked away. "No. And no one else ever has either."

Damon smiled. "Well, the boys in Providence, Alabama must be either blind or stupid."

"Stop. Girls like Racheal Parson and Brittny Booth are beautiful. Not me."

"I mean, yeah. If you go for the Hollywood model type with perfect hair and well-rounded figures, I guess they're alright." Damon nudged her shoulder, laughing.

"Yeah, they're alright. That's why every guy in school is thirsting after them like wolves."

"Not every guy," he replied.

Tamira looked up at him and smiled. "You're sweet. There's a very real possibility that you might need glasses, but you're sweet."

"I can see just fine." He cleared his throat before adding, "And I like what I see right now."

Tamira blushed, putting her hands over her face. How could he think she was pretty? It was hot out. Her cheeks were probably red and splotchy. The wind had been pulling at her hair all morning. "I probably look like a hot mess."

He reached out and gently pulled her hands from her face, taking them in his. "I'm not a guy who can do poetic speeches or whatever. All I know is that when I see you, my stomach ties itself in a knot and I feel like I'm going to throw up."

"I make you want to puke?" she said with a laugh. "Wow, and you said you're not poetic."

"You're killing me here. I'm trying to tell you something, and I don't even know what I'm trying to say."

"You're right. I'm sorry. Continue."

"You just make me feel good when I'm around you. It's weird and I don't even know what to make of it myself. I just really like being with you."

Tamira smiled. "I think you said it perfectly."

Damon swallowed hard as he leaned closer to her. His hand slid out and touched her cheek an instant before his lips met hers.

Tamira's brain went blank when she realized what was happening. His hand was on her cheek. He was moving closer. His eyes were closing. Her heart leaped into her throat and the air around her felt like she was in an oven. He was going to kiss her.

His lips met hers and her body froze, paralyzed by the flood of emotions, and questions. Why was he kissing her? It meant he liked her, liked her, didn't it? Should she close her eyes? Yes. Close them, you idiot!

When Damon pulled back, looking into her eyes, she smiled at him. Before she realized what she was doing, his cheek was in her hand, and she was caressing it gently.

"Was that okay?" he asked quietly.

"It was amazing," she cooed, still touching his cheek.

Damon smiled. "I mean, was it okay that I kissed you?"

"Oh," Tamira replied, blushing with embarrassment as she retracted her hand. "Yeah. I guess it's okay." She cleared her throat and looked away. "I-I didn't mind."

"Good," Damon said with a smile, "Because it *was* amazing."

Tamira closed her eyes and drew in a deep breath through her nose. She blew it out slowly and ran both hands over her hair. So far this was the best day of her life. Her heart was pounding in her chest and overflowing with feelings she never thought she'd feel. Her body tingled, and her mind was struggling to align her thoughts. Damon liked her. Like boyfriend/girlfriend liked her. He was wonderful and amazing and perfect, but he would also complicate her life in ways she'd never had to consider before.

Her smile vanished as the thought of her mother's reaction came crashing into her mind. In an effort to keep her safe, she barely let Tamira go to school. Having a boyfriend meant the possibility of dates, which meant being away from the house more. That would never do with her mother. She'd go through the roof.

"Are you okay?" Damon put a hand on Tamira's back.

His touch was like electricity but in a good way. "Huh? Uh, yeah. I'm good." She wasn't aware that she'd leaned forward on the bench. She forced a smile and leaned back, landing against the back of the bench with his arm across her shoulders.

He looked at his arm, then at her, and smiled. His expression asked if it was okay. When she didn't protest, his smile widened.

Tamira sank into the bench with a sigh. "I need to tell you something." She sat her hotdog on the bench beside her and looked at him.

"Okay. I kinda figured this was too good to be true."

Her heart sank with the sadness in his voice, then leaped with the idea that he thought she was too good to be true. She forced another smile for his sake then looked across the park. The fountain in the lake caught her attention for a second, but it couldn't hold it.

"My mother will not let me have a boyfriend."

"Is that what we are? Boyfriend and girlfriend?" he asked.

"I thought that's what you wanted. I mean, it's okay if you don't. I just-"

"I do," he said, cutting her off. "If that's what you want." Damon smiled at her.

"I do, but my mother doesn't."

"Why? She doesn't even know me."

"It's not you, it's any boyfriend. She doesn't like for me to go out."

"Like on dates or in general?" he asked.

"Like at all. She never leaves the house anymore and doesn't like for me to either." Tamira shook her head. "She barely lets me go to school."

Damon stared at her, puzzled. "Is it a thing, like when people are afraid to go outside?"

"Agoraphobia? No." Tamira shook her head. If that were all it was, she'd consider herself lucky. "Well, kinda, but not exactly. It's complicated." Tamira chewed on her bottom lip. "I'm worried that after a while it'll be too much, and you'll bail."

"Why would I bail?" he asked, caressing her shoulder with his fingertips.

A shudder ran through her as his fingers touched her through her shirt. She moaned quietly then shook her head, clearing the excitement of his touch.

"My life is incredibly complicated. My mother is very…" she waved a hand in front of her as she struggled for the right word. She finally settled on "protective."

"That's okay."

"You don't know my mother."

"Well," he began. "If I'm going to be your boyfriend maybe I should meet her."

"No!" Tamira gasped. She watched Damon recoil at the urgency in her voice. Closing her eyes, she took a deep breath. "I mean, she would never allow it. She doesn't let people in the house. It's complicated."

"You said that already, like three times," he said, nodding. "Look, parents are weird. Who knows why they do the things they do? It'll be okay. We can figure it out."

"I wish I were as confident, or it were that simple. You just don't know what I know."

"So, tell me. Don't you think we should go into this being open and honest?"

"I haven't told you anything that's not true." I just haven't told you everything, she added to herself.

"I know, but it feels like there's a lot that you haven't told me."

"It's complicated," she said with a sigh.

"That's number four. I get it. It's okay. I don't want to pressure you." Damon removed his arms from around her and rubbed his hands together. "Look, let's not put pressure on each other. Okay? Let's let this be what it wants to be."

Tamira swallowed hard, fighting back a wave of emotion. "I want to be your girlfriend."

"I want that too." Damon nudged her with his shoulder.

Tamira rubbed her face with both hands, sighing. How could she let this thing between them progress without telling him who she was, what she was? It was unfair to him, to them both.

"Look, Damon. I'm a-" her words froze in her throat. She couldn't bring herself to tell him. He'd surely freak out and walk away. How could he not? She was weird enough, but how could she tell him that she was a glass girl and not expect him to freak out?

"You're what?" he asked.

She looked at him, searching his eyes. "I'm different."

"I know," he said smiling. "I think that's what I like about you."

Tamira forced a smile, shaking her head as she looked at him. His big brown eyes were on hers and his smile melted her again. My god, she thought. This boy's going to break my heart in a million pieces. But until he does, I'm going to love every second of this.

Chapter Five

Tamira stood in front of the mirror in her bedroom holding her hair atop her head. She looked down at the picture of the model and sighed. She let her hair drop and turned the page with a moan. It was hopeless. She'd never be able to make her hair look like the women in the magazine. They were beautiful and had a professional stylist. It was hopeless.

Tamira looked up as a soft knock came at her door. Before she could answer, the door opened, and her mother stepped out of the dark hallway. The walls of her bedroom erupted with sparkling, multi-colored reflections that mirrored her mother's movements.

Crystal grimaced, shielding her eyes from the light streaming in through the open blinds. "Tamira, sweetie, must you always have these open? You know I don't like it."

"I'm sorry," she replied, watching her mother cross the room and close the blinds, sinking the room into shadows.

Crystal sat on her daughter's bed and watched Tamira cross the room herself and partially reopened the blinds. She noted the minor rebellion with an eyebrow arched but said nothing.

"Mama, I need some light."

"What are you doing? You've been up here all evening." She paused then added, "Since you came back from the library."

Tamira tensed but tried not to show it. She'd made up the library story. If she'd asked her mother to go to the park, with a boy, she'd have said no. "Nothing really. Just goofing off."

"Are you thinking of getting a new hairstyle?" She asked, eying the open magazine on her daughter's dresser.

Tamira shrugged. "I've thought about it."

Crystal shook her head, sending glittering streaks of light across the room. "Come sit by your mother."

Tamira sighed and trudged across the room. She moved to sit on her mother's left side, but a hand stopped her.

"On this side," she said. "Please."

"No, Mama." Tamira took her mother's hand and sat down beside her. She looked at the two-inch-long fissure on her left cheek that dominated her face. Jagged edges of glass lined the scar, revealing an open wound that resembled the inside of a broken geode. Tamira looked at the multi-faceted points of fragmented glass and smiled.

"You know mama, I've always thought you were so beautiful."

"Stop it, Tamira." Crystal looked away, covering the break with her hand. "I'm broken and you know it."

Tamira tugged gently at her mother's hand. "No, you're not. You're beautiful."

"You're a sweet girl," Crystal said. "But I have a mirror too. I can see what I look like."

"Okay, you have a blemish. You're not perfect. Big deal."

"It's not that, Tamira, and you know it." Her fingers danced along the wound carefully.

"Mama, even diamonds have inclusions. Isn't that what your mother used to say?"

Crystal smiled, remembering her mother's words. "There are inclusions, and there are breaks, sweetie. This isn't an imperfection."

Tamira rubbed her eyes. "Do you remember before, when we used to go places and do things?"

"Of course, I do, Tamira."

"It feels like a lifetime ago."

"It was six years and eight months ago. You were little. You probably don't even remember them."

"I was nine, Mama. I remember more than you think."

Crystal's hand went to her face again as her mind went back to the night she'd never forget. "I was careless, and your father was drunk. It never should have happened."

"But it did, momma. And you survived."

"That's all I did." She sighed and stood from the bed. "Look, this is not why I came up here, Tamira. I don't want to talk about it anymore."

"Mama, you can't spend the rest of your life hiding. There are things you can do. It's possible."

"Stop it, Tamira. I don't want to talk about it. You don't understand."

"I don't understand how scared you are? Really? In case you forgot we're just alike. I'm as much glass as you are."

"Well, you'd do better to act like it and stop taking so many risks."

"And hide in the dark forever? Mama, there's nothing to be ashamed of."

"Ashamed?" Crystal asked. Her head snapped around to look at Tamira, throwing blades of light across the room. "Is that what you think this is? Vanity?"

"Isn't it?" Tamira asked. Fear rose in her chest as the weight of her mother's stare fell on her.

Crystal pursed her lips and sighed through her nose as she stared into her daughter's eyes. Frustration welled within her, but she beat it back.

"You've never been broken, Tamira. In large part because I've devoted my life to protecting you. Sometimes even from yourself. A fracture in glass can never be fixed. Sure, it can be repaired, or covered up, but it'll always be there. Once you're broken, you'll always be broken."

"I know, but-"

Crystal put up a hand to squelch her daughter's protest. "It was my face that hit the corner of the table and broke, but it could just have easily been my back or my neck. I could have shattered, Tamira."

"I know, Mama," Tamira replied. This wasn't the first time she'd heard the story.

"I'm not sure you do." Crystal cradled her daughter's chin in her hand, lifting it to look into her eyes. "You're so beautiful, Tamira. You're flawless, just like I was. Pop Pop made sure of that. I just want to keep it that way."

"I need a normal life, Mama. I can't live like this."

Crystal thumbed a tear from her daughter's cheek. "I know you do, sweetie, but that's something not available to us."

"Why not? I'd rather be normal than perfect!"

Crystal nodded slowly. "Is that why you lied to me?"

Tamira's eyes dropped to the floor as the fire left her argument. There was no way the mother could know for sure that she'd lied. She'd have to rely on her reaction.

Tamira drew in a deep breath and raised her eyes to her mother's. "I don't know what you're talking about."

A wry smile pulled Crystal's lips. She was sure that Tamira had lied, but she was putting up a good front. "Did you go to the library?"

"I did," Tamira lied, holding her mother's gaze.

"What did you reference?"

"Osteogenesis imperfecta," Tamira said, invoking the name of the disease Damon thought she had. "It's also known as Brittle Bone Disease if you're wondering."

Crystal shook her head, her eyes moving to stay on her daughter's defiant stare. "That's an interesting topic."

"It's quite fascinating, actually," Tamira said defiantly.

"I'm sure it is." Crystal rose from the bed, breaking eye contact with Tamira. She went to the small desk in front of the drawn shades, casually flipping the pages of Tamira's notebook. Her eyes found a small heart in the corner of one of the pages. Inside the heart were the letters DK. She drew in a breath and closed the notebook.

Turning, she met her daughter's gaze again. "Tamira." She shook her head. "My sweet, beautiful little girl."

"I'm not a little girl anymore, Mama."

Crystal nodded as a sad smile came to her lips. "Oh, I know that sweetie." Crystal shook her head. "Where have the years gone?"

"Time waits for no man."

"Or woman, apparently." Crystal nodded, lost in thought. "I trust you, Tamira. I know you'll do the right thing. You're risking everything every time you go outside. It could all be over like that." She raised her hand to snap her fingers in front of Tamira's face but didn't. She shook her head and dropped her hand. "You know how quickly things can happen." Her eyes found her daughters and held them a moment. She smiled, nodding slightly, then walked across the room.

Crystal opened the door and turned back to her daughter. "You're a smart girl, Tamira. You'll figure it out. There are things worth the risk, and there are things not worth the risk. Once you're broken, you'll never be the same again. If you survive at all, that is."

Tamira watched her mother close the door, leaving her alone. She went to the window and flung the blinds up. Sunlight poured into the room as she spun and stared at the door. Her mother was probably still there. She'd see the light under the door. It was as much rebellion as she dared.

Good, she thought, seething in anger. She was tired of the shadows. Tired of hiding. Tamira clenched her fists as anger welled up inside her. She looked around, wanting to punch something. Knowing that breaking her hand would only prove her mother's point, she shook her fists in the air with a frustrated grunt as she paced the room.

Her mother was right about one thing, there were things worth the risks. If something happened and she fell, or broke, or even shattered into a million pieces, it would be worth it. She'd never felt so alive, so special. The simple act of thinking about Damon made her heart flutter with excitement. Damon Kennedy was definitely worth the risk, and it didn't matter what her mother thought.

Catching her reflection in the mirror, Tamira paused. Turning, she stared at herself, surprised that there was a smile on her face. Her fingertips touched her cheeks, making sure it was real.

She dropped her hands and sighed, still looking at her reflection. Her mother was right about another thing too. They weren't like other people. She wasn't like other girls. Whether she liked it or not, she had to play by a whole different set of rules.

Reaching out, she tapped the mirror with the tip of her index finger. The hard clink of glass on glass resonated through the room, reminding her of who she was. Like her mother, she was made of glass and there was no denying it. For her, every trip was a potential disaster, every fall could reduce her to pieces. Whether she liked it or not, that was a harsh reality that she couldn't forget.

Tamira swallowed hard as her fingertips went to her left cheek. Like mom, she thought. Tamira closed her eyes, pushing tears onto her cheeks as she remembered her mother's break.

She was young when it happened. She didn't see it, but her mother had told her the story as a cautionary tale many, many times.

They were celebrating her father's promotion at work with martinis. Music was playing, they were happy. It was a perfect night until it wasn't.

Her father caught her mother returning to the den after a trip to the bathroom. He knew her secret. He knew she was made of glass, but he must have forgotten, probably because he'd been celebrating all afternoon.

"Come give the district manager a kiss," he said, embracing her. He lifted her from the floor and spun her around. Her mother resisted, protesting his recklessness. He spun her several times anyway before setting her back on her feet.

Dizzy from the spinning, and probably the alcohol too, she stumbled. He moved to her, suddenly realizing what he'd done, but it was too late. She staggered a few steps, unable to regain her balance.

Turning as she fell, she put her hands out to catch herself. She knew they'd break, but it was better than shattering. But her hands didn't break. Somehow her husband had crossed the room in time and gotten a hand beneath her, arresting most of her fall. Her momentum shifted beneath his grip and her face glanced off the edge of the coffee table.

The sound of glass shattering filled the room, telling her that something had broken. She sat on the floor and looked at the tiny fragments of glass. They were split between the surface of the table and the floor beneath it.

Crystal watched one trembling hand reach out. Her fingers slid through the shards, still not knowing where they came from. She rubbed the pieces of herself between her thumb and fingertips, watching them fall to the floor in a glittering stream.

Another hand appeared before her. She checked the knees and legs sticking out of the short skirt she wore. They were intact. Finally, a hand went to her face, and she felt it.

She was broken. Her face was broken.

Tamira sighed again and dropped her hand. Even in the safety of her own home, with the man she loved, her mother had been broken. How could she expect to have anything close to a normal relationship with anyone with this specter hanging over them?

Damon didn't even know her secret. The truth alone would probably be enough to drive him away. What teenage boy would want to date someone like her?

Tamira turned from the mirror, not wanting to see herself. Tears streamed down her face as she began to sob. It only hurt because she'd let herself hope. She'd let herself fall for this boy despite knowing what she was. Worse than that, she'd let him get close enough to like her as well.

She could deal with her own pain and disappointment. She was used to it. But she couldn't stand the thought of hurting Damon. He was truly a nice guy. He was smart and funny, and for some unexplainable reason, he liked her. The longer she let this thing continue, the worse it would be when he found out; the more it would hurt the both of them.

Standing outside her daughter's bedroom door, Crystal froze when a wave of light suddenly swept across the floor. It flooded in from behind her, overcoming her in the dark hallway. She knew Tamira would open the blinds when she left. She always did. But this was different. This time she'd thrown them open in anger and frustration. The strain of her solitude was weighing on her.

Her eyes danced around the newly formed shadows and tears welled in her eyes. She knew exactly how her daughter felt. Her mother had kept her hidden in the name of safety. She'd lived through years of solitude, broken only by her mother, then her husband, and now Tamira. She hadn't asked for this life like Tamira hadn't, but it was the one they'd been given. They were made of glass. It was simply the way things had to be. It was a necessary unfortunateness that they had to bear.

They were made of glass, and glass breaks.

She took a long, deep breath and exhaled slowly through her nose, gathering herself. She closed her eyes, letting her fingertips find the scar on her cheek.

Knowing first-hand how quickly it could happen, how could she not do everything in her power to protect her only child, her precious little glass girl? She was beautiful and flawless, perfect. How could she not fight to keep her safe, even from herself?

Her mind went back to the arguments she'd had with her mother. Tamira was subdued compared to her own younger self. Once, after catching her sneaking out, her mother had locked her in her bedroom. When she snuck out the window and climbed down a rose trellis, her mother had bars installed on the windows. Eventually, she'd run away with Tamira's father and married. In the years that followed, and until her mother's death, their relationship never recovered.

Dropping her hand, she looked over her shoulder when her daughter's desperate sigh drifted into the hallway. Things were changing between them. Tamira wasn't a little girl anymore, and now there was a boy in the picture. She was young and in love for the first time. She knew from experience that tumultuous days lay ahead.

Crystal shook her head and wiped a tear from her cheek. No, she thought. Things weren't changing between them. They'd already changed.

Chapter Six

"Good morning."

Tamira's heart leaped when she saw Damon's smile. Every ounce of her being wanted to run to him and throw her arms around him. She wanted to hold him and feel him, just to make sure he was real; to make sure all of this was real.

Her eyes dropped to the daisy in his hand and the knot that had been in her stomach all morning tightened. She drew in a deep breath to control the wave of tears welling behind her eyes.

"Hi," was all she could manage to get out of her dry throat.

"I got you something." Damon held the flower out to her. "It's not much." He watched her stare at the flower but make no move to take it. "I just thought, maybe you'd like it."

Tamira looked into his anxious eyes, then back at the flower. It was the first time anyone had ever brought her a flower, and it had to be him. She studied the expression on his face, wanting nothing more to kiss his worries away. She wanted to leap into his arms and stay there forever, but she couldn't.

The fight with her mother had driven home a few unsettling realities. She'd been glossing over the fact of who she was, pretending that it wasn't a big deal. It was.

She was made of glass! A fall would literally break her into pieces! That couldn't be glossed over.

"Are you allergic or something? I'm sorry. I didn't even think about that." Damon lowered the flower. "I'm sorry."

The disappointment and sadness in his eyes broke her defenses. What should have been a sweet, beautiful moment had been destroyed by who she was. She gasped as tears began to pour down her cheeks. Damon rushed to her side and put an arm across her shoulders, leading her to the edge of the sidewalk.

"I can't do this. I'm so sorry." Tamira fell against him sobbing.

Damon looked around for a place to go that would afford them some privacy. He held her to him and led her to the end of the block. They turned the corner and walked to a brick alcove in front of Rosburg's furniture store. The store didn't open until nine. No one would be there this early.

Tamira sat down on the tiled steps, hiding her face in her hands as she sobbed.

"What happened? Did I do something?" Damon asked.

Tamira shook her head. "No," she said through her hands.

Damon sat down beside her. "Can I help with anything?"

Tamira shook her head again.

Damon looked at her. Not knowing anything else to do, he rubbed her back and let her cry. His mind reeled, trying to figure out what had happened. Surely this wasn't all over a flower.

"I-I'm sorry," Tamira said through her hands.

"It's going to be okay." Damon leaned forward and looked at her. He extended one crooked finger and wiped a tear from the back of her hand. "I don't really like daisies either. Personally, I think they stink. I saw a thing that said the only thing people hate more than daisies are karate movies and cancer. I don't even know what I was thinking."

Tamira laughed through her sobs and shook her head. "Don't look at me," she said, turning away from him. "I must look a mess, not that it would take much."

"Stop." Damon rubbed her back. "You look perfectly fine."

"B-bless your heart. I'm such a basket case. I-I wouldn't blame you if you ran away and didn't look back."

Damon shrugged. "I didn't sleep well last night. I think I'll just sit here and rest awhile." His hand moved to her hair, watching it slide between his fingers.

Tamira wiped tears with the heels of both hands and sighed, struggling to get herself under control. "I'm sorry."

"For what? Crying?"

"For everything."

"What'd you do?" Damon asked laughing.

Tamira shook her head and looked away. It wasn't what she'd done, but what she hadn't done. She'd deliberately kept her secret from him. Every day they were together, she'd lied by not telling him. "You don't want to be with me. You're a nice guy. I'm just too damaged."

"Stop. If I didn't want to be here, I wouldn't be here." His hand slipped beneath her hair, gently massaging the back of her neck.

Tamira moaned lightly and leaned back against his hand. "Feel any better?' he asked quietly.

"Mmm-hmm," she moaned, closing her eyes as the tension left her body.

"Good."

A shudder racked Tamira's body, making her shake all over. "Look," she said, regaining her composure. "You should be heading to school. You'll be late because of me as it is. I don't want you to get into trouble."

"I'm good," he said, rubbing her back again. "You'll be late too."

Tamira shook her head, drawing a hitchy breath. "I'm going to go back home. I can't do school today. Mom will write me a note."

"I don't have to go to school either. I think I feel something coming on," Damon added two dry coughs for effect.

Tamira smiled as she wiped the last of her tears away. "You're going to get in trouble. I appreciate it. I really do, but you should just go. I'm not worth the trouble."

Damon shook his head and slid his arm around her shoulders. "I wish you'd stop saying stuff like that."

"Like what?"

"That you're 'not worth the trouble' or that you're 'damaged'. That's not how I see you at all." He gave her a quick squeeze. "I think you're pretty great, in case you haven't noticed."

Tamira took a deep breath, regaining some composure. "Well, we can't just sit here all day."

Damon looked around the deserted side street and shrugged. "We probably got a little while."

"The flower was sweet of you," she said, leaning into him. "Thank you."

Damon looked around but couldn't find the flower. "I must have dropped it. Sorry. I just thought…" He shrugged as his voice trailed off.

Tamira groaned as she drug the hair from her face. "I'm such a mess. I bet you don't make that mistake again."

"I know, right? Steal a flower from an old lady's yard and your girlfriend has a mental breakdown."

"Wait. You stole the flower?"

"I prefer to consider a floral liberation, thank you very much."

"You were going to give me a stolen flower?"

"It's the thought that counts, here," he said laughing. "Let's concentrate on that."

Tamira looked at him, amazed at how easily he could make her feel so much better. Just his presence lifted her spirits. Sitting in the morning sun, she thought him the most wonderful thing that she'd ever seen.

"Uh, you got a little something…" Damon touched his nose with a bent finger.

Tamira wiped her nose. "Oh, God. How embarrassing. I'm so sorry."

"It's alright." Damon shrugged. "I wish I had a napkin or something for you. He pulled up the tail of his shirt and offered it to her.

Tamira waved him off, turning away as she cleaned her nose. "Why are you not running for the hills? My God, I'm such a freak."

As she turned back to him, Damon moved in quickly and kissed her. He held his lips to hers for a few seconds, then drew back. He smiled at her and said, "That's why."

Tamira ran both hands over her hair and clasped them behind her neck. She looked skyward, letting her head fall back with a moan. Why was he making this so hard for her? Everything would be easier if he would just run away.

"I'm sure you can find prettier girls who'll let you kiss them."

"I don't want to kiss pretty girls," he said laughing. "Just you."

"Wow. That'll get the old self-esteem machine chugging. Thanks."

"I'm playing. Actually, I think you're the most beautiful girl in the world." His fingers gently brushed a lock of hair from her face. "I could look at you all day."

"Like watching a train wreck?"

Damon shook his head and smiled. "No. Like watching an artist paint."

"You poor thing." Tamira shook her head. "Your vision's getting worse by the day."

"I can see just fine."

Tamira stared into his eyes, swimming in the adoration within them. How is this even possible, she thought? How is this beautiful creature looking at me this way?

He hooked Tamira's pinky with his. "You feeling better now?" he asked, his voice soft and comforting.

Tamira nodded, sniffling. She offered a delicate smile. "I am. Thanks to you."

Damon shrugged. "Well, something tells me that I'm the reason you cried in the first place so…"

Tamira shook her head. "Not even close."

Damon's eyes searched her face, searching for an explanation.

She cleared her throat and looked away, avoiding his inquisitive eyes. "I should get going."

"Wait." He took her hand. "We're already going to be late for school. Why don't we just cut?"

"No. Are you crazy?" Tamira shook her head. "We'll get caught and we'll both be in trouble. My mom's just looking for an excuse to make me stay home."

"C'mon. I know some places we can hang out and no one will see us. We can chill for the day and relax. You seem stressed, maybe a break will help some." Damon smiled at her. "Then just go home after school like nothing happened."

"They'll call our parents."

"No, they won't. Why would they care? We're not in grade school." Damon put a hand over hers, sandwiching it between his. "I don't care anyway. I just want to be with you."

"Your parents must not be like my mother."

Damon looked at her, both eyebrows wiggling playfully. A wide grin slid across his face. "It'll be fun," he said, dragging out the "u" sound in fun.

Tamira shook her head. "I should probably just go home."

"Look, I'm already tardy. My folks won't get much madder about this if they even find out. Anyway, if you went home now your mom will be asking all sorts of questions."

Tamira nodded. He wasn't wrong. She closed her eyes and drew in a deep breath. This was exactly the sort of thing she was worried about. If she went anywhere but school, the risks would be compounded. She didn't even know where he wanted to go. Anything could happen.

When she opened her eyes and saw Damon's sly smile, she knew she'd go with him. Her heart climbed into her throat as the decision solidified in her mind. She knew better, but at the moment there wasn't any place she'd rather be than with him, wherever that ended up being.

"If I go with you, you have to promise me something."

"Anything."

"First of all, we have to be careful. I mean, very careful. We can't be going anyplace dangerous."

"Okay, cool, cool," he said with a grin. "There goes the tour of the gasoline and match factory, but whatever. We can do that anytime."

Tamira laughed, nudging him with her shoulder. "Say it."

"I promise. Nothing dangerous."

"Good." She nodded curtly. "And..." she dropped her gaze to the sidewalk, blushing. "This doesn't mean I'm going to... you know."

Damon stood quickly and threw his hands into the air. "What? Forget it then. I outta here." He watched Tamira's shock grow. When she opened her mouth to speak, he broke out in laughter. "I'm joking." He sat down next to her again "It's a joke."

"I'm serious."

"Okay," Damon conceded, his smile vanishing. "None of that stuff. Fine." He rubbed his palms together and looked at her with a grin. "But what if I'm overcome with the desire to kiss you? Is that allowed?"

"Really? Overcome with desire? What do you read at night?"

"What? I'm just saying."

"Well, if you're *overcome with desire*," she said, doing her best impression of a proper southern lady. "I guess it'll be okay. But only if you're *overcome with desire*. Not just, like, wanting to a little bit."

Damon held out his hand. "Deal."

Tamira shook his hand, laughing. "I don't want you kissing me to be just a thing we do. It should mean something. Every time. Shouldn't it?"

"You're right," Damon began, "I agree. You're a great girl. Kissing you should be a big deal."

She nodded. "Thank you."

"You know," he said looking at her with a sly grin as he fanned his face with his hands. "I'm starting to feel a little hot, like a little overcome right now."

Tamira stood quickly, avoiding him. "Control yourself, you beast." She watched him tumble to the platform she'd been sitting on. They shared a laugh as he leaned back on the stoop, staring up at her.

He cocked his head to the side and smiled. "You're really very pretty from this angle."

Tamira rolled her eyes and smiled. She looked down at him and shook her head in disbelief. How was it that he thought she was beautiful, and no one else ever had?

"Come on. Are you going to lounge about this place all day? Because there was mention of some magical setting that you wanted me to see." She extended a hand down to him.

Damon laughed as she pulled him to his feet. "C'mon. Let's get outta here."

Chapter Seven

Tamira put her bare feet in the water and smiled. The creek rushed past a few feet away but was calm and still in the eddy that formed behind the boulder she sat on. It was cool and refreshing on a day that was turning out to be warmer than expected.

In the back of her mind, she kept hearing her mother's voice, but every time Damon looked at her, it got quieter. She'd never done anything like this. It was dangerous, she knew, but it was also amazing.

"Like it?" Damon asked, returning from using the bathroom behind a nearby tree.

"It's absolutely beautiful," she said, surveying the canopy of trees above them.

Damon smiled as he sat down. "I can't believe you never came down here. The guys said everybody comes here in the summer."

Tamira shrugged, paddling her feet in the water. "I told you that I don't get out much."

"Yeah, you did." Damon slipped his feet into the water beside hers. "But you never said why."

"I don't know. It always seemed so dangerous. I've told you about my mother, right?"

Damon smiled as he slid his foot against hers. "I know, but it seems a bit excessive to me."

Tamira shrugged, her eyes watching her feet move in the water. "When you thought I might have that brittle bone thing, what did you think?"

"It sounded like it would suck."

"Yeah, that," she conceded with a chuckle. "But what did you think about me when you thought I had a disease like that? Did it make you not want to talk to me anymore?"

Damon shook his head, "Na. I don't think it did. I was really just trying to figure out why you were, like, ultra-careful. Maybe I just wanted to know more about you. I don't know."

"If I did have it, would we be here now?"

"I feel like I should say yes so I'm gonna go with yes."

She nudged him with her shoulder. "Seriously. Just tell me the truth."

Damon shrugged. "I don't know. I mean, I like being with you. You're pretty and smart, and funny. You also have impeccable taste in men."

She laughed, shaking her head.

"I like to think we would, but I wonder if you'd be here."

"Me?"

"Yeah, you. If your bones could break so easily, I doubt if you'd come way off down here."

"Maybe I would if the opportunity arose to be with someone special."

Damon smiled. "Still."

Tamira sighed. "Would you treat me differently if I did have that? Or something like that?" she asked.

He looked at her for a moment, then smiled. "The first time I saw you something about you just stuck with me. I can't even explain it." He looked down at the water. "I mean, you were pretty, but there was just something about you." He shrugged. "You moved all graceful and smooth, like a cat, you know. I don't know. It's weird, but I just knew that I wanted to know you."

"I'll bet your friends had a fit about that."

Damon shrugged. "I guess. You know, being a guy isn't the easiest thing in the world. I mean, sure I'm rocking it, but it's complicated too."

Tamira laughed, leaning against him "For the record, you are rocking it, by the way."

He smiled. "Thanks. You know, approaching a girl is hard. It's stressful, especially in front of other people. I think a lot of guys just act like jerks because they think they're supposed to."

"Well, Brady Dennis and Easton Brooks have a natural talent for it, if you ask me."

"I can't argue with you about that. They're idiots. They just happened to be some of the first guys I met when I moved here. My mom kinda pushed us together. My dad is Brady's dad's new boss. I guess my mom wanted to make friends as much as I did."

"It must be hard moving to a whole new state."

Damon nodded. "Yeah. You don't know anybody or know where anything is. Everything is different than back home. We lived just outside Indianapolis. Moving to Providence, Alabama was a bit of a culture shock. It hasn't been easy."

Tamira slid her foot against his. "Did you have a girlfriend back in Indiana?"

Damon shrugged. "I don't know if you'd call it that."

"What would you call it?"

"I don't know. Things were different." He reached out and hooked her pinky finger with his. "She wasn't like you."

Tamira smiled. I'd bet the farm on that, she thought. "Was she pretty?"

"The guys said she was, but you never know."

"Is she prettier than me?" Tamira asked, regretting the question as soon as she asked it. She looked away, putting her hand up. "Never mind. Do not answer that."

Damon bent forward so he could see Tamira's face. His eyes searched hers for a long time before he smiled. "Not even close."

She shook her head. "Thanks for lying."

Damon laughed. "Seriously. She wasn't. To be honest, she was hideous. Her name was Gladys. She had this big wart on the end of her nose with a hair growing out of it."

"Gross," she laughed, giving him a playful push. "Stop."

Damon let the laughter die. "You're beautiful, Tamira. I wish you could see what I see."

She turned away, blushing. Tears welled in her eyes as a wave of raw emotion washed over her. "Thank you."

"You don't think you are, do you?"

"I'm not." Tamira shrugged, looking at the water. "On a good day, I'd rate myself as tragically average."

Damon shook his head. "Well, I disagree one hundred percent."

"Why do you think I'm pretty? Nobody else ever has."

"Maybe they're used to seeing you. I don't know."

Tamira lifted a foot from the stream, watching the water run down it. "I'm scared."

"Of what?"

She put her foot down and lifted the other one from the water. "I'm scared that one day you won't think that anymore."

Damon shrugged. He opened his mouth to speak but closed it. He gently brushed a lock of hair from her face and looked at her. "I don't know what the future holds. There's no way to tell. It is scary. Maybe someday you won't like me anymore. We're teenagers. Things change."

"That's what scares me. Things do change."

"Yes, they do." His eyes watched a leaf float by, pushed by the current. "But, you know, being scared of what might happen won't stop things from changing. Sometimes things change and end up better than they were. Change is inevitable. It shouldn't stop us from enjoying the things that are happening now. Should it?"

Tamira sighed. "It shouldn't, but sometimes it does."

"It won't if we don't let it."

Tamira looked at him and smiled. She wished he already knew her secret; that he knew she was a glass girl and still wanted to be with her. She closed her eyes and looked away, fighting back tears.

Damon touched her chin and gently turned her back to him. He took his time with the kiss, lingering against her lips. When he drew back, she was crying.

Sliding his hand to her cheek, he thumbed a tear from her cheek. "What do you want to tell me?" he asked, almost in a whisper.

"It will make you not want to be with me anymore."

"You don't know that."

Tamira nodded, wiping another tear. "I do know. That's why I haven't said anything. Nobody knows this about me."

"Nobody?"

"Not a living soul in this whole stupid town except my mother."

Damon searched her eyes. "Did something happen? Did somebody hurt you?"

A sad smile came to her lips as she shook her head. "It's nothing like that at all."

"You can tell me, Tamira. It won't matter. Not to me."

"Damon Kennedy, you're the first boy who's ever acted this way toward me. You're sweet, kind, handsome, and I can't understand why you're here with me, or even give me the time of day, really."

"Because you're sweet, kind, and handsome too. Well, not handsome. More like beautiful. You know what I'm saying. That's why. I like being with you. I can't stop thinking about you."

Tamira sighed. Every time he spoke to her it made things more difficult. Every time he looked at her with those brown, soulful eyes, she wanted to not be the girl she was.

"I'm not ready yet," she said. "I just can't bring myself to say it. All I keep thinking about is the look on your face when I tell you, and you walking away, calling me a freak."

"Do you think I'd do that?"

"I don't know that you won't. We've known each other for just over a week. And if you did, I don't know if I could handle it."

Damon shrugged. "A week and a half, but it feels like a lot longer." He ran a hand through his hair. "I can't stop thinking about you, Tamira. It's crazy, I know, but I can't help it. It's like you're a magnet or something, pulling me to you. I can't even imagine anything that could make me act like that."

Tamira clasped her hands in her lap and looked down at them. That was just it. No one would ever even imagine anything like she was. The possibility that a girl could be made of glass wasn't even in the realm of logical thought. She was a living, breathing anomaly. Of course, he couldn't imagine something like that.

"Look. Don't tell me then. Don't ever tell me. Let's just enjoy this thing we have now and don't talk about it. Like I said, we're teenagers. We don't know what the future holds. We don't have to worry about that. Just let things be what they are and enjoy it."

Tamira smiled. It was easier for him. He wasn't hiding who he was.

"Besides," he said with a smile, "Maybe I got a deep, dark secret too."

"Okay," she said, dragging the word out. She splashed water on his foot playfully. "Whatever."

"No, really. It's, uh, it's really deep and really dark and really secret." He nodded. "It's downright life-altering actually."

"Wow. It must be a heavy burden to bear," she said with a grin.

"You have no idea. Lotta weight." Damon patted his shoulder. "Lots."

Tamira laughed. "Well then. Since we both have a secret. I guess that makes us even."

"And I'm not going to tell you, so don't ask." Damon crossed his arms and looked away, holding his chin high in the air.

"Fine then. Don't tell me."

"You can stop begging. I'm not going to tell."

"Keep your goofy secret," she said, poking him in the ribs. "It's probably lame anyway."

"Stop," he said, fending off her hands. "It's not lame. What it is, is deep and dark."

"You already said that," she said, tickling him. "And life-altering."

"Stop. you're going to make me fall in." Damon grabbed her hands and pulled her to him. He tried to kiss her lips, but she turned her head. When he tried again, she turned it the other way.

"Are you *overcome with desire?*" she asked, laughing.

"I'm way past that. I was overcome with desire the first time I saw you and it hasn't let up yet."

Tamira lent in and let him kiss her. While their lips were together, she drew in a deep breath. The smell of his body wash and the heat on his skin mingled to form a divine, intoxicating scent that invaded her body, causing her stomach to turn a flip.

She felt his hand on her knee but decided not to deflect it yet. If it moved too far north, she'd stop him. During the long kiss, it moved a little, but not far enough for her to intervene. Her mother said that boys always wanted to push the limits of what girls would allow, but he hadn't crossed that line. Yet.

After the kiss, Damon leaned back on the rock, resting on his elbows. He smiled at Tamira and nodded for her to join him.

She looked down at the rock and cringed. Normally, she wouldn't be caught dead anywhere near something like this. As it was, she'd been forced to find a smooth, flat spot to sit on and be very careful with her movements. As much as she wanted to lay back on Damon's chest, it was too dangerous.

Tamira shook her head. "Sorry. It looks very uncomfortable."

Damon sighed and looked around for a better spot. "What about there?" He pointed to a mossy patch next to a towering oak tree. "That looks soft."

Tamira surveyed the area and grimaced. "I don't know."

"I'll check it out." Damon leaped to his feet and sprung from the boulder. When he landed hard on the ground, Tamira put a hand to her chest. It still amazed her that people could do things like that without a care in the world.

Damon patted the moss in a silly, exaggerated motion, then motioned for her to join him. "There are no peas under this mattress, my princess."

"What?" Tamira asked, carefully making her way off the boulder.

"Like the Princess and the Pea story?" He asked, his hands spread out before him. "From when we were little? You don't remember the story?"

Tamira shrugged. "I got nothing."

Damon flopped onto the moss and leaned against the tree. "There was a girl who claimed to be a princess. They did a test and said a princess was so delicate that she could only lay on the softest of beds. So they stacked up like fifty mattresses and she slept on them. The next day they asked how she slept, and she said awful. The king said you can't be a princess then. But it turns out a maid had hidden a pea under the bottom mattress, and she could feel it. Maybe she had some kind of sleep disorder. I don't know. It was a while back."

Tamira stared at him, wide-eyed. "Wow. That's quite a reading list you got there. First, it's cow blood and murder, now it's royalty and vegetables." She climbed carefully from the boulder and made her way to him. She sat on the bright green moss beside him.

"It was like second grade or something. Our teacher probably read it to us."

Tamira nodded, as she checked the ground around her. "Sounds like I dodged a bullet on that one."

"Well, this is Alabama. You guys probably read a different version," he said with a grin. "Maybe the Trailer Park Princess and the hubcap."

"Now you're talking," she laughed. "That's some top-shelf literature there." Confident in the safety of the moss, Tamira settled in beside him. His arm slid around her, and she laid her head on his chest.

After a long silence, Damon said, "This is nice."

Tamira nodded. "It is nice." She watched her fingers dance on his chest. "I wish we didn't have to go back."

"We don't. We can stay here forever. Live in a cave. Maybe get some animal skins or something. You'd look good in a leopard skin I bet."

"No," she said, shaking her head. "Redheads can't wear orange. I think I'm more of a zebra skin gal."

"Zebra?" he asked. "You know how hard it would be to kill and skin a zebra?"

"Easier than a leopard?" she laughed. "At least a zebra doesn't have claws. Plus, a leopard runs like sixty miles an hour."

"But just short distances," he replied, laughing.

"Oh, well, that's different then." She patted his chest. "Let's just stick to getting clothes from the mall for now."

"Okay then. Suit yourself. Your loss." Damon pulled her to him and smiled when she snuggled in against his chest. He knew he was still smiling, but he couldn't help it. He'd never been with anyone like her. She seemed to really get him and could banter better than any girl he'd ever known.

"I'm glad you hated my flower."

"I didn't hate your flower. It was beautiful." She watched as a bird fly across her field of vision and let out a contented sigh. "I'm sorry I ruined your moment."

Damon squeezed her. "It's okay. I've had a lot better moments today." He thought for a moment. "I could steal you another one tomorrow."

"That's okay."

"Seriously. I'll rip the whole bouquet out of the ground. Not roses though, because of the thorns. But any other flower and I'll snatch them suckers right out of the ground. That's the kinda guy I am."

"Let's spare the little old lady gardeners some heartache and just say the one was plenty." She looked up at him. "Okay?"

"I can't be held responsible for what I do when I'm in the throes of a crime spree for my woman."

"No more thievery, Damon Kennedy." She tickled his ribs. "Promise me."

"Okay. Okay," he said laughing.

"Say it. Say the words." She rose off his chest, tickling his ribs harder.

"Okay. I promise. No more flowers." Damon grabbed her hands as she moved to tickle him again. He rolled over, moving to position himself over her.

Tamira felt their weight shift. She sank to the moss, and he moved next to her. When he leaned in to kiss her, she felt something hard beneath her left hip. She pushed up against him to alleviate the pressure, but he'd committed to the movement. His body met hers, pushing it harder against the ground.

"Ouch!" she exclaimed, as something in her hip cracked. "Stop. Let me up." She clambered from the ground, staring back down at the moss as a hand went to her hip.

"What happened? I'm sorry. What?"

Tamira's heart was in her throat. She didn't know what to say, what to do. She was too afraid to look at her hip, but she knew something had happened.

"I have to go home," she gasped. "Now."

"Okay. Are you okay?" Damon took her hand as they started down the path. "What happened?"

"There must have been a rock or something under the moss." Tamira put a hand to her hip. Through her clothes, her fingers found a small divot that hadn't been there before. Her breaths started coming in panicked breaths as they moved quickly along the path.

"I'm so sorry. Are you hurt?"

"It's not your fault," she said, fighting back tears.

"I'm so sorry. Can you walk? I can carry you."

Tamira nodded. "I'll be okay. I just have to go home." Her mother's voice came to her as they made their way along the path. "I told you," the voice in her head scolded. "Now you're broken."

She put a hand over her mouth as tears began to flow. She's right, Tamira thought. I am broken.

Chapter Eight

Crystal Brannigan looked down at the wound on her daughter's hip and sighed. It was bound to happen eventually with the risks she took. She was just glad it was minor, and in an easily concealed spot. Maybe, she thought, this will teach her a lesson and the cost won't be as high as her own.

She looked up at her daughter's sobbing face as she lay on her bed. The corners of her mouth sank. All the years of carefully watching had gotten her nearly grown before she suffered a break. She hated to see her so upset, but she knew the feeling too well.

"It's okay, sweetie. Mama will fix it."

Tamira opened her mouth to speak, but another bout of sobs consumed her.

"Do you want me to come back when you're feeling better?"

"No," Tamira sobbed. "Fix it now."

Crystal pursed her lips and shook her head. The story Tamira told her wasn't very believable, but she was sticking to it. She might have believed a slip in the Home Economics class if her daughter had come home with her shoes on.

"Okay, sweetie. Lie as still as you can." Crystal pulled the light stand closer and bent over her daughter. The wound wasn't large, about the size of a dime but elongated. Fortunately, it wasn't very deep. She'd only lost a sliver off the surface. It looked like the result of bumping a desk, as Tamira said, but it almost assuredly wasn't.

Crystal opened the bottle of resin carefully and applied a few drops to the milky surface of the wound. Sitting the bottle aside, she took out a brush and carefully smoothed the resin. When she'd finished that, the picked up a small felt rag and wrapped it around her fingernail. She traced the perimeter of the area, making sure there wasn't any resin outside the wound.

"You'll have to lie still for an hour, Tamira, to make sure the resin cures properly. We must ensure it doesn't splinter."

Tamira wiped tears from her cheeks. "I'm sorry, Mama."

Crystal looked at her daughter and sighed. "This didn't happen to me, Tamira. It happened to you. I'm the one who's sorry."

"It's not your fault."

Crystal stopped backing the repair kit in its case and looked at Tamira. "Then who's fault is it?"

Tamira shook her head but didn't say anything.

Crystal finished repacking the kit and set it aside. She lifted a blanket and covered Tamira, making sure to leave the wound and her bare hip exposed.

"You're upset, sweetie. We'll talk when you've rested some. Try to get some sleep." She turned and walked to the bedroom door. "Do you want me to leave the light on or turn it off?"

"Off."

Crystal switched off the light and slipped out the door, closing it behind her.

Tamira relaxed, freeing her emotions. She'd contained most of them in front of her mother but needed to let them out. Her mind was reeling uncontrollably, flip-flopping between embarrassment, anger, frustration, and pain.

Lying in bed in the dark room, her eyes went to the tiny slivers of light creeping around the heavy drapes. Why did this have to happen to her? Why today? How had the best day of her life turned so suddenly to the worst?

As a young girl, she'd been plagued by nightmares in which she fell onto something hard and shattered into a million pieces. As she grew, the fear subsided, but it never completely went away. It would take a major fall or something catastrophic to shatter her. She'd learned to avoid the most dangerous situations, but she'd dropped her guard with Damon. Now she had a break.

Tamira closed her eyes, overwhelmed by all the thoughts fighting for attention in her head. She knew now why her mother preferred to sit in the dark.

Tamira trundled down the steps, favoring her left leg slightly. It didn't hurt, and her mother's repair would keep it from splintering further, but she didn't want to take chances with it so soon.

The emotional storm she'd endured yesterday wiped her out and she ended up sleeping through the night. She'd awakened naturally at six this morning, her regular time on a school day.

She stifled a yawn and wiped the sleep from her eyes. Two steps from the bottom, she stopped suddenly. Her eyes locked on the shoes she'd worn yesterday, now tucked neatly under the narrow table beside the front door.

She looked around the foyer, but it was empty. Had she worn them home? She didn't have them on when she was sitting with Damon. Her sleepy mind couldn't remember. Surely in the chaos of the incident, she'd forgotten them. Or had she? If she had forgotten them, who brought them home?

Damon.

Tamira's mouth fell open and her heart skipped a beat. It had to be Damon. No one else would know whose shoes they were and certainly wouldn't have brought them home if they knew they were hers.

That meant Damon was here. That meant he met her mother! "No. No. No," she whispered as she hurried down the steps and into the foyer.

"Tamira."

Tamira wilted when her mother's voice floated in from the sitting room. Her chin dropped to her chest. "Yes, Mama."

"Did you sleep well?"

"I did." Tamira crept to her shoes and squatted. She slid her fingers into them and stood quietly.

"How do you feel?"

"Much better." She turned and started for the steps. Maybe if she could hide the shoes upstairs her mother wouldn't mention them. "Thank you, Mama. You're the best."

"Tamira," her mother called, the whisper of a laugh in her voice.

"Yes."

"Can you come in here?"

"Okay, Mama." Tamira screwed up her face in frustration as she tiptoed to the staircase. She reached to put her shoes down on the steps.

"You can bring your shoes with you."

Tamira's head fell back, and she moaned as she turned. She walked into the sitting room, the sneakers dangling from her fingertips.

"You're feeling better?" Crystal asked.

"I am. Thank you so much."

"Come in. Sit." Crystal patted the sofa next to her.

Tamira wanted to do anything but, yet she complied. "I guess the break wasn't as bad as I thought. It's just a chip, really."

Crystal nodded. "It wasn't bad." She paused, staring at her daughter. "This time."

"Mama, please."

"Tamira, what am I going to do with you?"

She shrugged but said nothing. It was usually best not to.

"I saw how upset you were yesterday, Tamira. Don't try to minimize this. It was minor, this time. It might be more serious the next time."

"Mama, I've been very careful. This is my first real break, and it was just a chip."

"That is true." Crystal conceded reluctantly. "But your behavior lately is lending itself to more of this. First the near fall on the sidewalk, and now this. One has to ask, what has changed?"

"Nothing."

"Tell me. Did you bump into a table in school?"

"Yes, mama."

"Barefooted?"

Tamira sighed, deflated. "Does it matter where it happened?"

"I don't suppose the where matters as much as the why. Now does it?" Crystal's left eyebrow arched slightly. "Or maybe we can ask who caused it?"

"I don't know what you're talking about," Tamira lied, looking around the room.

"Tamira, sweetheart, your mother wasn't always as old as I am now. I was once a young girl too you know."

Tamira sat in silence, fingering the laces on her shoes.

"I know there is a young boy, Tamira. I don't know his name, but I know what he looks like."

Tamira's head sprung up.

Crystal smiled. "Yes, he's the one who brought your shoes home. You were already asleep. He crept up the sidewalk just after dark and left them by the door where you'd surely find them when you went out. Strange that he wouldn't ring the bell."

Tamira shrugged.

"I can only assume you told him of my reservations about you seeing him."

Tamira dropped her gaze to her hands to hide the smile she couldn't stop from coming to her lips. He'd gone all the way back just for her shoes and brought them home, leaving them where she'd find them.

Crystal let out a worried sigh. "Is he the same boy from the sidewalk?" She watched her daughter nod her bowed head. "I suppose he is a classmate of yours." Again, her daughter nodded but said nothing. "Does he have a name?"

Tamira looked up, her eyes finding her mother's. If she told her his name, her mother might get him in trouble. But did she dare defy her mother so openly?

Crystal watched the struggle in her daughter's eyes for a moment then shook her head. "Is he nice?"

Tamira smiled, glad that her mother wasn't pressing the issue. She would, eventually, but she'd have time to warm her to the notion before that came.

"He is nice, Mama. And sweet, and he's kindhearted."

Crystal sighed again. The light in her daughter's eyes told her she'd already lost the battle. "Oh sweetheart, come here." She opened her arms.

Tamira fell into her embrace. "He's perfect, Mama."

"Does this boy with no name feel the same way about you? A girl must be careful in these matters, you know."

Tamira shrugged and smiled at the same time. "I think he does. It seems like he does."

"How long have you known him?"

"Since the first day of school. He's new."

"I take that to mean that he doesn't know about us. About you."

Tamira shook her head against her mother's chest.

"It's a big thing not to know, Tamira."

The image of Damon pretending to have a "deep, dark secret" swam into her mind and Tamira smiled. She pushed up from her mother's chest and sat beside her on the sofa.

"I told him there was something about me. Something big, but I wasn't ready to tell him yet. He was fine with it. He said I didn't have to tell him anything."

Crystal reached out and stroked her daughter's hair. Her shoulders fell with a groan. "Oh sweetie, this isn't

100

like a shoplifting charge or something that happened in the past. This is who you are, Tamira. What you are. It'll always be there, affecting everything you do." Crystal's hand went to her daughter's hip. "Like this."

"I know." Tamira shook her head. Damon not knowing her secret was what lead to her chip. If he'd known, they probably wouldn't have been there. That was part of her reluctance. If they'd not gone to the creek, a whole day of beautiful memories never would have happened. "I just don't want him to treat me different. I just wanted to be normal."

"You are different, sweetheart. We both are. No less, just different. You know that. It can't be avoided or denied."

Tamira started to cry again. "I'm just afraid that if I tell him, he'll go away, Mama. It's been so wonderful."

Crystal smiled, thankful for her daughter's chance to have the experience. "Will it be any easier to tell him in a month? Two months?"

"No." Tamira wiped her cheeks. "But if I wait, I'll have more time to enjoy this."

"Do you think that's fair, Tamira?"

"That's another thing. If I tell him and he does run away, he might tell everyone in town."

Crystal chuckled. "Do you think he would do that?"

"No," she admitted. Even if he chose to not be with her, Damon wasn't malicious. He'd never do anything to deliberately hurt her.

"Besides," Crystal added, "Who would believe such a crazy thing? A girl made glass. They'd think he was crazy."

"I don't want that to happen either, even if he does run away."

Crystal smiled. "You do like him, don't you?"

Tamira nodded emphatically. "A lot. Like, a lot, a lot. Mama. He's not like anyone I've ever met before."

Crystal let out another heavy sigh. The sparkle in her daughter's eyes was beautiful to see. For so many years they'd been dull and lifeless. "I don't suppose there's a chance you'll stop seeing him if I ask you to."

Tamira looked away, avoiding her mother's watchful stare.

"That's about what I thought." She smiled and hugged her daughter to her again. "I love you, sweetheart."

"I love you too, Mama."

Crystal wiped a tear from the corner of her eye. She'd tried so hard for so long to protect her, but at what cost? Tamira wasn't grown like she was. She'd never experienced love and the warmth of a man's touch. There was so much she'd missed out on in the name of protection.

Her fear for her daughter was hers, not Tamira's. She couldn't force a young girl to carry the weight of a woman's fears. It was unfair. She'd protected her this long. Now she was going to have to step back and let Tamira protect herself.

And yet, she thought with a sigh. This one boy had stormed the walls she'd built around her daughter and found her perfect gem and made her fall for him. Maybe, she'd only hid her daughter until the right person came along.

"This boy must be very special."

"He is, Mama. I can't even…" Tamira's emotions overcame her, and she began to cry again. She wiped tears from her cheek and nodded. "He is."

"Are you in love with him?"

"I don't know what it feels like to be in love, Mama. I've never been in love before." Tamira drew in a hitchy breath. "But if it's more than the way I feel now, I think it'd kill me."

Crystal smiled. Her little girl was in love.

"Well," she said with a sigh. "I suppose if you're going to go traipsing through God knows what with this boy-" Tamira started to deny it, but her mother held up a finger to stop her- "I cleaned the mud off your shoes last night dear. You're not fooling anybody."

Tamira dropped her gaze, conceding the point that they'd been traipsing through something.

"If he's going to be in your life, I suppose I should meet this dreamy young man who is stealing my baby girl away from me."

Tamira looked up, shocked. "Really? You're not going to make me stop seeing him?"

"At this point, I'm quite sure it wouldn't do any good. Maybe if you have a place to hang out, you'll be safer. Lord knows I don't want you climbing down a rose trellis."

"What?"

"Never mind. Just invite him to dinner."

Tamira squealed with joy. "Oh, Mama. You should see him. He's gorgeous. And he smells like this chocolatey, musky thing that you just want to eat."

Crystal cleared her throat. "Excuse me?"

"Not like that," Tamira said, blushing. "You'll see. He's, he's just scrumptious."

"Scrumptious?" she asked, laughing. "You know this whole thing scares your poor mother half to death, don't you?"

"Me too, Mama. It's like I'm about to explode. I'm scared he'll really, really like me. I'm scared that he won't. I'm scared he'll run away if he finds out. I'm scared he won't. It's been driving me crazy. Yet through it all, all I can think about is him and his smile, and his thick wavy hair, and the way he looks at me." And his lips, she added to herself.

Crystal smiled. She hadn't seen Tamira this happy in years.

"Mama, I've been busting at the seams to talk to you about all this. His name is Damon Kennedy and he's just gorgeous."

"I'm glad to see you so happy, Tamira. I am, but don't you think this is a little fast?"

"I don't know, Mama. I've never had a boyfriend before."

Crystal forced a smile, but her heart broke for Tamira. She'd sheltered her from so much. "Just be careful. Okay?"

"I am. I mean, I can't help feeling like this. I tried not to, Mama. I did. I even tried to get him to not walk with me."

"Really? What happened?"

Tamira shrugged, dropping her eyes to her hands. "I couldn't do it. I just couldn't ask him to stop. I know it complicates things, Mama." Tamira sighed. "I spend half my time scared to death and the other half smiling like an idiot. This might be my only chance. I just couldn't let it pass me by."

Crystal gave her daughter a knowing smile. It hadn't been so long since she was young and in love that she couldn't remember how it felt. Unlike her own mother, she wasn't going to try to lock her daughter in a tower and hide her from the world. Not anymore at least.

"Okay," Crystal stood and put her hands on her hips. "If you're going to have a boy over, we'd better get started cleaning this place up. How does Friday night supper sound?"

Tamira clapped, smiling broadly, but her joy faded quickly. Like everything else in her life lately, this was a double-edged sword. She was ecstatic that her mother wasn't going to forbid her from seeing Damon, but if he came over, he'd meet her. That meant he'd see her break.

"Don't worry, sweetie," Crystal said, reading her daughter's face. "I'll cover it up. I'll wear a bandage and say I had a mole removed or something." She smiled. "It won't matter. He's not coming to see me."

"Are you sure that it's okay?" Tamira went to her mother's side.

"It's fine."

Tamira reached up and cradled her mother's left cheek in the palm of her hand. "You know I think you're beautiful, Mama."

"I know you do sweetie." Crystal hugged her daughter. "I know you do." She took a deep breath to combat the wave of tears behind her eyes. One escaped and rolled down her cheek. Catching the light from the window, it sent a lone, tiny rainbow onto the wall.

Crystal followed it down the wall until it faded, leaving them both standing in the shadows.

Chapter Nine

Tamira stood in front of the mirror in her bedroom, staring at her reflection. The burgundy skater dress hung on her thin frame well, and even somehow managed to accentuate her nearly non-existent breasts. She ran her fingertips over the lace sleeves and smiled. It was the prettiest dress she'd ever worn.

Her mother knocked on her bedroom door as she opened it. She was in a bathrobe and her hair was wrapped in a towel. "You're already dressed?" she asked with a smile.

"I know. I couldn't help it. It was just hanging there, begging me to put it on."

Crystal stood behind her daughter, looking at her reflection in the mirror. "You're such a beautiful young woman. I'm sorry I've not helped you see that before now."

"It's okay mom." Tamira smoothed the dress and smiled, looking at her reflection. She couldn't believe how much her life had changed in the short time since school started.

"You ready to start on your hair?" Crystal gathered her daughter's auburn locks and held them atop her head. "You still like the idea of wearing it up? Or did you decide down?"

"I like it up, but maybe down is better. For tonight."

Crystal smiled. "Smart girl. Up would be too formal. The poor boy would probably think he was at the prom." Crystal leaned over her daughter's shoulder, catching her eyes in the mirror. Her eyes narrowed. "And we don't want him thinking this is a senior prom."

"Mom." Tamira blushed at the insinuation.

Her daughter's reaction lifted a burden from Crystal's chest. She didn't have to worry too much about anything physical happening with this boy. Yet.

"C'mon. Slip your dress off and we'll fix your hair. You're going to be so beautiful."

"Mama." Tamira caught her mother's hand as she turned to retreat to the bathroom. "Thank you so much for everything."

"You're welcome, but it's my pleasure."

"I don't just mean the dress and inviting Damon over. I mean everything. My whole life, all of it."

Crystal smiled. "You're the best daughter I could have ever asked for, sweetie. You deserve all of this and more."

"You know," Tamira began with a sigh. "I've been thinking. All my life I've been afraid. I've been scared of falling. I've been afraid of breaking. Honestly, I still haven't gotten over those dreams from when I was little, the ones about shattering. For a long time, I hated myself."

"Oh, baby." Crystal hugged her daughter. "Don't say that."

"I mean. I hated being who I was. I hated being glass. I used to wish I were somebody else, anybody else. I used to daydream about running and playing with the other kids."

"I know, baby. I know." Crystal sighed. Like Tamira, she hadn't asked for this life, but it was all she'd ever known.

"Lately though, I've started to realize that we're amazing. We're this wonderful, crazy, unique blend of nature and Pop Pop's craftsmanship and some strange magic and nobody else in the world can say that. Nobody. Just me and you."

"We're just two peas in a pod."

Tamira laughed. "Maybe like a ceramic pod with glass peas that sits on a shelf."

Crystal laughed. "Well, you're not sitting on a shelf anymore. C'mon. Let's get your hair done, unless you want your mother answering the door in her bathrobe."

"He's just a kid mom. I don't want to scar him for life." Tamira ushered her mom into the bathroom.

"Now that I think of it, a bathrobe and some pink fuzzy slippers does sound comfortable. Maybe with a cigarette hanging in the corner of my mouth and a can of beer."

"No," Tamira laughed. "I will run away and join the circus."

"What? No? I'm warming to this ensemble."

Tamira laughed. Tonight was shaping up to be even better than Monday at the creek. Tonight, she felt like a regular girl, and it was wonderful.

Damon got out of his parent's car and stepped into the August heat. He looked at the sun, still high in the sky at six P.M., and instantly started sweating into his dress shirt. He clutched a small box of chocolates for

Tamira's mother in one hand and a bouquet for Tamira in the other.

He looked over his shoulder and ushered his parents off. His mother rolled down the window and snapped another picture of him with her phone.

"Mom," he pleaded in a whisper. He waved the flowers toward the street, begging them to leave. Turning, he took a deep breath and started for the front door.

Crystal called her daughter to her bedroom window. "Come here, come here. This is a very telling part."

Tamira joined her at the window and peered down at the sidewalk. Her heart leaped into her throat when she saw Damon.

"Watch how he comes to the door. It'll tell you if he truly likes you or not."

Halfway down the sidewalk, Damon gathered the gifts in one hand then smoothed the front of his shirt and adjusted his tie. He switched the gifts to the other hand and did the same with his left hand. The chocolates slipped, but he trapped them against his body with his elbow. Sure that they were secure, he took the opportunity to run a hand over his hair.

The box slipped from his arm. He moved to catch it but dropped the flowers. He threw his hands into the air before picking them up. He took a deep breath and continued to the door.

"Aww," Crystal cooed. "He is scrumptious."

Tamira nodded emphatically. "Isn't he though?" She leaned closer to the window, watching as he neared the door. He took another deep breath and extended a hand to the bell but hesitated. He took a step back and shrugged his shoulders. He closed his eyes and took another deep breath.

"What's he doing, I wonder."

Crystal smiled. "He's probably saying how lucky he is that such a beautiful girl is letting him come for dinner."

Tamira rolled her eyes and smiled, shaking her head.

"He's probably just giving himself a pep talk. Guys do that kinda stuff. He's like, 'You got this' or 'you the man'." Crystal flexed her arms in front of her, grunting.

Tamira laughed, turning her attention back to Damon. He stepped toward the door and extended a hand.

Inside the house, the doorbell chimed. Tamira looked at her mother with wide eyes. "Oh my God." She started for the bedroom door, but her mother stopped her.

"You stay here. I'll answer the door and call for you. Don't yell down the stairs. Don't even say anything. When I call, you count to fifty and slowly make your way to the sitting room."

"Mom," Tamira pleaded.

"Trust me, Tamira." She smiled at her daughter and nodded. "Fifty, and don't be fast about it."

"Hello, there. Damon, I presume."

Damon felt his throat go dry. He stood motionless, staring at the woman before him in awe. She was tall and thin, like Tamira, but her long blonde hair was pulled up in a tight bun atop her head, revealing a slender neckline that gave way to a full bosom. Like her daughter, she was strikingly beautiful.

He cleared his throat but still couldn't speak. He extended the box of chocolates to the woman. His eyes followed her as she leaned forward and took the box from his hand.

Crystal smiled at him, thankful to have someone look at her that way again, even if it was a kid. She intentionally turned to her right, revealing the bandage on her left cheek. It seemed to break the boy's paralysis and he finally spoke.

"Yes, Ma'am. Damon Kennedy." He extended his free hand to shake hers.

Crystal shook his hand and invited him in. "What a thoughtful young man. Thank you so much."

"Yes ma'am. You're welcome."

"Tamira is running just a little late, please excuse her." She motioned to the sitting room. "You can wait in here if you like." Crystal deposited him on the sofa in the living room and returned to the staircase. She called for her daughter, then went back to the check on Damon.

"So, Tamira tells me you go to her school," she said, sitting in a chair next to the sofa.

"Yes ma'am. Providence high. We're both freshmen."

"Yes, I know." Crystal smiled, appreciating the boy's nervousness.

"Do you have any classes together?"

"Just one. We're both in-"

Crystal smiled when his words stopped suddenly, and his face flushed. His eyes widened, staring at something behind her. She followed his gaze to Tamira, now standing in the doorway.

"Ah. Here she is," Crystal said, standing. She watched Damon stand and lumber nervously across the room. He smiled and extended the flowers to her daughter. She fought back a wave of emotions as her daughter's beautiful face lit up. Her eyes were sparkling, and her face could barely contain her smile.

Despite her joy, sadness crept into her heart. Tamira had crossed a line and would never return. She'd found someone to love. Nothing would ever be the same for either of them again. Her little girl was a young woman and her grasp on her was fading quickly.

She looked at her brave, independent daughter and saw so much of herself. Tamira was smarter than she was at her age, more worldly. She just hoped it would keep her safe.

"If you two will excuse me, I need to go and check on supper." Crystal kissed her daughter on the cheek. "I hope I can stay out of these chocolates Damon brought me. What a thoughtful young man." Crystal opened the box and smelled them. She looked at Tamira and smiled. "They smell positively… scrumptious."

Tamira's eyes grew wide, and her face flushed. "I think I heard a timer going off," she said through her embarrassment. "In the kitchen."

Crystal smiled. "I better go check. You two be good now." She shot Tamira a quick wink before leaving.

"What was all that about?" Damon asked, grinning nervously.

Tamira shook her head. "My mom's weird. Sorry. C'mon." She took Damon's hand and lead him back to the sofa.

"I know I'm taking a chance with a whole bouquet, seeing how you reacted to one daisy."

Tamira laughed as she turned the bouquet upside down. "No roots. I guess you didn't pass any untended gardens on your way over." She laughed and nudged him with her shoulder. "But seriously, they're beautiful. Thank you."

"You look amazing," he said, his eyes washing over her.

"Thank you. You're handsome all cleaned up."

"Thanks." Damon tugged at his tie. "Seriously though. You look-" he shook his head as he took her in, "-beautiful."

Tamira smoothed the dress across her lap. "Thank you, again. Do you like the dress?"

"I do," he said, nodding eagerly.

"It's called a skater dress. I've seen other girls wearing them in school."

"I've never seen any that looked like that." Damon fidgeted on the couch. "Can I tell you something?"

"Sure."

Damon wiped the sweat from his brow. "You remember that whole 'overcome with desire' thing?"

"I do think I remember something about that," she said coyly, putting a finger to her chin.

"Tamira, you look so beautiful. If I don't kiss you right now, I might just die."

She smiled and leaned closer to him. "Well, I wouldn't want you to die."

Damon leaned in closer, staring into her eyes. His heart thundered in his chest. A bead of sweat collected between his shoulder blades and ran down his back. Suddenly his tie felt very tight around his neck. As he closed his eyes in preparation for the kiss, he felt himself drifting to his left, but couldn't stop it. He was vaguely aware that he should have felt Tamira's lips by now, but he couldn't see. Darkness closed in and he felt himself falling.

"Damon? Are you alright?"

Damon opened his eyes. Tamira was leaning over him. Her wide eyes were staring down at him in shock.

"What?" He looked around, finding himself reclining on the couch. He shook his head and sat up.

"Are you okay? You don't look so good."

"I'm good," he lied, still trying to figure out what happened and play it off at the same time. Whatever it was, it only lasted a few seconds.

"Did you faint?" Tamira asked. She wanted to laugh, but she needed to make sure he was okay first.

"No," he insisted, shaking his head.

"I think you fainted," she said, a smile creeping to her lips.

"I didn't faint."

"It's okay."

"It was probably this tie. It's cutting off circulation to my brain. It's too tight. I can barely breathe." He slid a finger beneath the tie and tugged at it.

"Okay," Tamira said, hiding a smirk behind her hand.

"I didn't faint."

"I said okay," Tamira said.

"It's not funny. I could have suffocated to death."

"You're fine." Tamira sniggered again.

Crystal popped her head into the room. "You guys about ready to eat?"

Tamira hopped up from the couch and extended a hand to Damon. "Do you think you can make it to the kitchen?"

"I'm fine," he replied, his cheeks now red as a beet.

Crystal looked at Damon, then at Tamira. "What did I miss?"

"Nothing much," Tamira said, crossing the room. "But Damon wanted to kiss me so bad that he fainted."

Crystal watched her daughter pass, then looked back to Damon with a questioning smile. "You okay, buddy?"

"I'm fine, ma'am. I did not faint."

Crystal patted him on the back as he passed her. "Don't sweat it, kiddo. It happens to the best of 'em."

"I didn't faint."

"You probably just need to eat something."

"I didn't faint."

Chapter Ten

"That was delicious," Damon said as he and Tamira walked back into the den after supper. "Your mom is a good cook."

"Thank you," she replied, carrying a vase containing the flowers Damon had brought. She put them on the coffee table and sat on the couch. "Isn't your mom a good cook?"

"I guess. We eat a lot of takeout. She can cook, she just doesn't like to."

"Oh," she replied with a shrug. "You can take your tie off now if you want." Tamira eyed him with a smile. "I wouldn't want you to faint again."

"And we're back to that." Damon shook his head and began loosening his tie. "I didn't faint."

"Okay, fine." She took the tie from his hands and slipped the knot loose. Holding each end, she pulled him closer and planted a quick kiss on his lips. "Feeling better?" she asked with a smile.

"Actually, I feel a little swimmy-headed. Maybe another kiss, just to be safe."

Tamira smiled and let him kiss her. When they parted, she sighed and settled into the couch. "I'm probably not supposed to say this, but I like kissing you."

"I like kissing you too." Damon settled in beside her and took her hand in his. "Thanks for inviting me over."

"I'm glad you came. My mom told me you seem nice. I told her you were an illiterate brute. You know, just to keep her guessing."

"Well, that should help a lot," Damon said laughing. "You want to watch some T.V. or something?"

Tamira shook her head and sighed. "Look, I wanna talk. Do you remember how I said I had a secret, and I couldn't tell you?"

"Yeah? Like my own deep dark secret?" he asked nodding.

Tamira rolled her eyes and laughed. "Yeah, just like that, but not made up."

Damon squeezed her hand. "And?"

"I think I'm ready to tell you."

"Are you sure? You don't have to."

"I think I do." Her eyes searched his face, planting the way he looked in her memory. If he reacted badly, she wanted to remember this moment. She dropped her eyes and sighed.

"What changed your mind?" he asked.

Tamira shrugged. "I like you, Damon." She tugged at the hem of her dress, unable to look at him. "I think you like me too. I mean, I don't think you'd lose consciousness for just anybody."

"I do reserve it for special occasions," Damon laughed. "Look, I know we haven't been together long, but it seems like a lot longer. I like you too, Tamira."

She looked up at him and smiled, buoyed by the look in his eyes. He meant what he said. "I just think you should know me. The real me."

"Unless the real you is secretly a wildebeest, I think we'll be fine."

"No." She pulled her hand from his and clasped them in her lap. "I'm not a wildebeest. But I am a glass girl."

The words flew out of her mouth before she could stop them. She squeezed her hands together tightly, bracing for his reaction. Tamira held her breath, keeping her eyes on her hands. She didn't want to see the shock and revulsion on his face. If he were looking at her the way she'd imagined he would, she'd just die.

After a painful silence, she forced herself to look up. He was staring at her blankly. He nodded his head like he was waiting for her to say something else, to explain something.

"I'm sorry," he finally said when she didn't. "I have no idea what that is. Is it like a Baptist or something? I don't know."

"You heard me, right?"

"I heard you say you were a glass girl, but I don't have a clue what that is so…"

Tamira shook her head and drew in a deep breath, deciding on a different approach. She turned to him and took his hands in hers. "Damon Kennedy, I am a glass girl."

He nodded. "Okay. Tamira Brannigan, I still don't know what that is."

She sighed and dropped his hands, turning from him.

"I'm sorry. I'm not from here. I don't know what a glass girl is." He put a hand on her back. "I'm sorry. Is it a local thing?"

She turned back to him. "Stop talking. Kiss me one more time before I explain this to you."

Damon leaned in and gave her a long kiss. "So far I like this secret thing."

119

"Stop talking again, please." She looked at the ceiling and drew in a long breath. She puffed out her cheeks as she exhaled. "A glass girl is exactly what it sounds like. I am a girl made out of glass."

Damon shook his head slowly. "Maybe I'm just stupid, but I still don't understand. You're made of glass? What does that mean?"

"Do you know what glass is?" she asked, frustrated. "Like windows and drinking glasses and well, glass?"

"Yeah," he said nodding. "Sure."

"Do you know what a girl is? Like, not a boy. I am a girl."

"A beautiful girl at that," Damon added, wiggling his eyebrows up and down.

Tamira shook her head. "You're not helping. I want you to think about the two words separately," she held her fists out with the index finger of each pointing to the ceiling. "Glass," she said looking at her left hand. "Girl." She looked at her right hand. "Now, put then put them together." She brought her fists together until her fingers stood side by side. "That's what I am."

Damon tilted his head to the side, looking at her. He opened his mouth to speak but closed it. He rubbed the back of his neck and scratched his chin.

"Your big secret is that you're a girl?"

"Yes. Made of glass."

"A girl?" he asked again.

"Yes."

"Made of glass?"

"Yes."

He sighed, running a hand through his hair. "Are you sure you're not just crazy? I mean, that might explain some things better than this."

"I'm perfectly sane. And I'm perfectly glass."

"A glass girl?" he asked, his brow furrowed deeply.

"Yes." She watched Damon sink into the couch. He scratched his head and looked at her inquisitively. She nodded. "Yes."

"A glass girl?"

Tamira nodded again, fighting the tears she was sure would come. "Do you want to leave now?"

"No," he said, his brow furrowed. "But I do have a few questions."

Tamira smiled, relieved. He hadn't run from the room. That was good. She settled back with him and took his hand in hers.

"I expect that you would."

"And you're sure you're not just crazy?" he asked again.

"Pretty sure."

"Okay, next question. Am I crazy?"

Tamira laughed. "The jury's still out on that one."

"But I am awake, and sitting in your house, and you did just say you were a glass girl?"

"Yes. Yes. And yes."

"Are you sure I didn't hit my head when I fainted?"

"I thought you said you didn't faint," she asked with a grin.

"Right about now I'm not so sure about anything." He rubbed his mouth and looked at her.

Tamira nodded.

Damon sighed. "And you're a glass girl?"

She nodded. "In the glass." She watched confusion spread across his face and laughed. "It's like 'In the flesh' but I'm glass so I went with the other thing."

"Glass?"

"Yes. Too soon? It was a corny joke. I'm sorry. This is a serious conversation."

"No. No. It was funny. I'm just still processing all the other stuff." He waved his hand in the air next to his head. "In a week I'm sure that'll be funny."

"A week?" she asked. "Does that mean you don't want to break up with me?"

He looked at her. "Was that another glass joke?"

"What?" she asked.

"Break- up with you? Glass, break. Get it?"

Tamira smiled. "No. Well, I guess it could have been, but I didn't mean it as one."

Damon squeezed her hand. "The answer is no. I don't want to cease the relationship with you."

Tamira's smile leaped across her face. "I was so scared you would."

"Well, I don't." Damon looked at her, shaking his head in disbelief. "A glass girl?"

"Yes," she said nodding.

"I mean, like, physically, how is that even possible?" He took her hand in his, rubbing his palm against hers. "You seem normal."

Tamira shrugged. "I wish I could explain it. I don't understand it either, to be honest." She pushed her free hand through her hair.

"Do you have superpowers?"

"Superpowers? No. Sorry."

"But you are made of glass?"

"Yes."

"But you look normal."

"Thanks, I think."

"Were you born this way?"

"Yes." Tamira sighed. "It's a long story."

"Well, I think in this situation, I'll make time to hear it."

"My grandfather was a glass artist."

"Seriously?"

Tamira nodded. "He loved glass. Everything about it fascinated him." She got up and went to a large cabinet against the wall. Opening the doors, she took out a figurine and brought it back to the couch.

"He was very famous for making these figurines back in his country. I never met him, but they say he made thousands of them. When he started one, he'd work until it was finished." She handed it to Damon. "Sometimes he'd spend hours and hours on one. They had to be perfect in every way or he'd melt them down and start over."

Damon examined the figurine, turning it over carefully in his hands. The glass was flawless, so clear against his dark slacks that it almost vanished. Bending closer to the lamp beside the couch, he looked at the face of the woman. The detail was unbelievable. His eyes narrowed. It was a perfect image of Tamira's mother.

"That's some crazy skills right there. Amazing." Damon handed it back to her, making sure she had it before letting go. He got up and went to the cabinet. He pushed the doors open and his jaw dropped.

"There must be hundreds of them. Are they all as good as that one?"

"There's six hundred and forty-seven. And yes, each one is flawless."

Damon looked at Tamira, stunned. "Your grandfather made all of these?" His eyes washed over the figurines. Each one stood on a polished wooden base before a sheet of colored glass, lending them color, and revealing the depth of the work.

"Every one of them," she said with a smile. "These are just the ones he had in his studio when he died."

"And you're glass too?" Damon asked. "Did he make you?"

Tamira smiled at the look of wonder on his face. "Nope." Tamira closed the doors to the cabinet and lead Damon back to the couch. "But he did make my mother, sort of."

"Sort of?"

Tamira took his hand again. She sighed and looked at the ceiling. "When my mother was born, they say Pop Pop- that's what everybody called him. He was born in a small mountain village in what my mom always called 'the old country'. Anyway, they said Pop Pop was over the moon because she was perfect."

"She's very pretty. I guess it's hereditary."

Tamira blushed. "Thank you. She was so beautiful that people on the street would stop them and remark how it was to be expected that an artist would create such a beautiful child. When she was two, something was going around, though. I can't remember what it was. Maybe measles or something. A lot of kids in the village caught it and died. My mother got sick. She developed a high fever. The doctors tried everything. I mean, her fever wasn't even measurable it was so high. They weren't poor, you know. Her parents tried everything. The doctors were surprised that she lived as long as she did, being so hot and all. Pop Pop was beside himself. He usually worked every day for hours and hours, but when his baby was sick, he didn't even fire up his furnace."

Damon rubbed Tamira's back as she wiped a tear from her cheek.

"I'm sorry. This story kills me every time."

"It's okay. Take your time." He slid closer to her, wrapping an arm around her.

"Pop-Pop sat up with her day and night for weeks. They said he didn't sleep or eat or leave her side for anything." Tamira sniffled and wiped her cheeks again. "When she finally died, he went crazy. People said you could hear his screams from miles away. He grabbed her little body and ran out of the house with her. He barricaded himself in his studio and stayed there for a long time."

Damon found a box of tissue on the table by the couch and handed them to Tamira. He waited patiently, rubbing her back, while she blew her nose and regained her composure.

"When he finally did come out, he was singing. I always imagined him drenched in sweat, you know. Maybe his hair was all messed up." Tamira smiled, running a hand through Damon's hair, "Like yours gets at the end of the day sometimes." She smiled, watching his hair slide between her fingers.

"Anyway, he was happy again. All he said was 'I saved her,' and then he fell dead."

"My God, what happened?"

125

Tamira wiped her nose with a tissue clutched in her free hand. "They figured it was exhaustion. The men in the village kept a watch on the furnace while he was in there and they said he worked day and night without stopping. They told my grandmother that he was chanting and saying stuff they didn't understand." She shrugged. "Like it was in a foreign language. I don't know."

"What about the baby? You said it was your mother?"

Tamira nodded. "It was. When they went inside the studio, he'd gotten the kiln so hot that it broke. There was broken glass everywhere. Different kinds, and shapes and colors all over the floor." Tamira sighed and shook her head.

"They found her on his workbench. She was perfect and alive just like before. Everyone said it was a miracle and the whole town celebrated."

"What did he do to her?"

"Nobody knows, but she was made of glass."

Tamira dug the tissues into her eyes. Damon held her tight to him while his mind did the mental gymnastics to make sense of what Tamira had told him. It all sounded like irrational gibberish and perfectly sane at the same time.

"I'm sorry." Tamira cleaned her face and looked at him. "Now do you want to run away?"

"How could I?"

"I don't know. You could stand up and just walk out."

"That would be the stupidest thing any guy ever did in the history of guys. And we've done some pretty stupid things." He took her hands in his. "I'm not going anywhere so stop asking."

Tamira sighed. "I guess you're wondering about me?"

"That's an incredible story about your mom, but yes."

Tamira sighed, gathering herself. "My mother grew up and got married to a man who owned a window washing company."

Damon's jaw dropped as he stared at her. "Are you messing with me?"

Tamira erupted in laughter. "I am. Sorry. I couldn't help it." She fell back on the couch, still laughing. "The look on your face was priceless though." She sat up, wiping a tear from her eye. "I'm sorry. He was a salesman. They had one baby, and it was me."

Damon reached out and cradled her face in his hand. He stroked her cheek with his thumb, studying it intently. She closed her eyes, pushing tears from the corners. He captured one on her right cheek with his thumb.

"I can't even begin to wrap my head around this."

Tamira opened her eyes, watching as he rubbed the wetness between his thumb and fingers. When he saw her looking at him, a smile slid across his lips.

"When I was a kid, I used to ask my mother lots of questions. It's a little hard to comprehend when you're four."

"Four?" Damon asked. "It's pretty confusing right now."

"I don't even understand it myself. I know it doesn't make sense, yet here we are."

Damon shrugged. "And you're made of glass?"

Tamira nodded. "Mama always would look at me and say, 'It's a gift from Pop Pop. Be grateful. Don't question the magic'."

"In a way, it makes sense," Damon said, looking into her eyes. "It would have to be magic to make someone as perfect as you."

"I don't know if you're being funny, or not. Are you?"

Damon shook his head. "Not even a little bit."

Tamira's eyes filled with tears and her chin began to quiver as she fought back a wave of emotions.

Damon moved in quickly, putting a hand on both sides of Tamira's face. He turned her to face him and pressed his lips against hers. He let the kiss linger for a long time, then hugged her tightly to him.

"I think I just fell in love with you Tamira Brannigan."

She smiled as tears ran down her cheeks. "What took you so long, Damon Kennedy."

Chapter Eleven

Damon reached for the doorbell but hesitated. He armed sweat from his brow and looked around. On the walk over, he'd convinced himself that last night never happened, or happened differently than he remembered. He'd been so swept up with emotion, he couldn't remember half of what they said.

Tamira told him she was a glass girl. He told her he loved her. She said she loved him. There was something about an old guy and magic. He massaged his forehead. Whenever he tried to make sense of it, it gave him a headache.

He sighed and extended his finger toward the bell but again stopped. What would he do if she acted like nothing happened? Would that be okay? Was he willing to take a step back? He'd used the "L" word. That was huge. And he meant it. That was even bigger.

How could he be in love with a girl made of glass? How could one even exist? They'd talked about the duality of being human, and glass. He'd asked questions, and she'd answered as best she could. If she didn't fully comprehend what she was, how could he?

Did it matter? How could he not be in love with Tamira? She was the same person he'd met and was drawn to. The same person he thought about constantly. The same person he'd fallen in love with. She'd been made of glass all that time. The only difference was now he knew.

Compounding the impossible situation, Tamira had come up with a plan for him to impress her mother, so she'd keep letting her see him. He moaned and shook his head. Everything was jumbled in his mind, and he wondered if it was all a dream.

He wiped the sweat from his forehead and sighed. Mustering his courage, he extended his hand to the doorbell again.

Crystal opened the door quickly. "Hey, kiddo."

Damon's mouth went dry. For a brief instant, he considered running away. He could just go home and pretend none of this happened. Just run! his mind screamed, but his feet refused to move.

"Are you alright?" she asked, her smile widening. "You look kinda pale. You're not going to faint again, are you?"

Damon dropped his gaze. "No ma'am. I-Is Tamira home?" he asked.

"She is," Crystal said with a smile. "Won't you come in?" She ushered Damon into the foyer. "She'll be right down."

"Thank you." Damon followed her to the sitting room. "Um, It's nice to meet you." He groaned, embarrassed. "I'm sorry. I mean, It's nice to see you again."

"You too," she said eyeing him suspiciously. "Is it hot outside? You're really sweating."

Damon wiped the sweat from his brow. "Yes ma'am. It's pretty hot, I guess. I mean, yes. It's hot. I'm sorry about your father."

Crystal stopped suddenly and turned to look at Damon. A strange, level smile parted her lips slightly. "Relax, kiddo." She shook her head and laughed as she led him into the sitting room. "You're going to give yourself a heart attack."

"Yes ma'am," he said, following her into the sitting room. He eyed the cabinet containing the figurines as he passed. Its presence reassured him that last night had indeed happened.

"I'm sorry." Damon sat on the sofa but didn't settle in. "I don't know what's wrong with me today. I'm kinda nervous. I didn't mean to blurt that out about your dad."

Crystal drew in a long breath and nodded. "I'll assume that Tamira told you about us."

Damon dropped his gaze, rubbing the back of his neck. "Is it all true? I mean about you and her?" He looked up at her, meeting her eyes for only a moment before dropping his gaze back to his hands. "I'm sorry. It's none of my business."

Crystal smiled. "Yes, Damon. It is true. All of it. As you can probably imagine, our life is somewhat complicated." She looked at the anguished young man before her, and her heart swelled for him. He seemed like A nice boy, and Tamira was already in deep over him. But feelings were one thing, being smart was another.

"Tamira couldn't explain how or why you all are glass. It's really hard to understand."

Crystal shrugged. "Look, I'm glass and I don't even understand it myself. It doesn't make sense. It violates the laws of anatomy, biology, and probably even physics.

I guess there are things in this world that aren't supposed to make sense."

Damon's brow furrowed deeply. "But you're people too, right?"

Crystal laughed. "What do you think?"

"You both seem normal enough."

"That's reassuring."

"I mean…" He rubbed the back of his neck, unable to look at her. "You know what I mean. You both seem normal, I mean, like regular people."

Crystal nodded. "I know it's a lot to take in at once, Damon. Do you want some advice?"

"Please."

"Just let it be what it is."

Damon nodded. "It's just so-" he searched for the right word. "Amazing."

"Damon," she said. When he looked up at her she continued. "We are what we are. There's no changing that. I'm glass. Tamira is glass too. We have to be careful who we let in. It's a big thing to welcome someone into our lives, but that's what we've done. Both Tamira and I."

"I know. It's a lot."

"You'd be well served to make sure you're prepared to be in Tamira's life. It won't all be hugs and kisses, you know."

Damon nodded. "I like her," he began awkwardly. "I really do, she's amazing." He hesitated, shifting his weight and cleared his throat. "But could anybody ever be prepared for something like this if they hadn't lived it? All I can promise is that I will do the best I can to make her happy and keep her safe."

Crystal stared at him, watching him shrink beneath her gaze. "That's a very good answer, Damon." She smiled and shook her head. "Almost perfect." She crossed the room and looked into the foyer. "Did he do okay, Tamira?"

Tamira appeared in the doorway dressed in a pair of black leggings and a pink tee shirt. "Oh, Damon's here," she said feigning surprise. "I didn't hear the bell."

"Knock it off, sister. The jig is up."

Tamira's shoulders drooped. "Dang. How'd you know?" she asked her mother.

"How did I know that you two knuckleheads rehearsed that?" Crystal laughed. "Oh please. First of all, I was a kid too, once. Secondly, Damon here was sweating buckets and he sounded like a robot from some old T.V. show."

Tamira crossed the room and took his hand as he stood from the couch. "Way to blow it, genius," she laughed.

Crystal laughed, stalking around the room with her arms in front of her like a robot. "I. Will. Do. My. Best."

Damon shrugged, laughing. "What did you expect? She's looking at me like she can see through me. But, just for the record, though. I mean it. I will do my best."

Crystal smiled. "I know you will, kiddo." She crossed the room to leave but stopped and turned back to them. "Because if you break my daughter-" She held her fists together, then broke them apart, eyeing him with one eyebrow cocked.

"Mom," Tamira pleaded.

Crystal paused in the door staring back at them. She was no longer smiling. Her eyes darted between them before she finally settled on Tamira. "Things are different now. I just hope we're all ready for the change."

Tamira watched her mother walk away and then groaned, turning back to Damon. "I'm sorry. I told you she was very protective."

"Don't be sorry. I don't blame her at all now that I know."

Tamira looked down at her hands as she went to the sofa. "Wow," she said, wiping her palms on her pants. "You really are sweating. Were you that nervous trying to get one over on my mom?"

Damon shrugged, watching her adjust the flowers he'd brought her yesterday. She'd arranged them in a vase and placed them on the coffee table. "It's just hot outside," he lied, deciding not to tell her how scared he was.

"She's right, you know. Things are different now that you know."

"It'll be better now. Now I know why you do things. And I can-"

"Help keep me safe?" Tamira interrupted sharply.

Damon shrugged. "I guess so. Isn't that a good thing?"

Tamira pointed a finger at him. "You look here, Damon Kennedy. I don't need another mother hen looking over my shoulder. Don't you go getting ideas of being in cahoots with my mother. You're my boyfriend and that's what I expect you to be. I've made it this long without a caretaker. I don't need one now."

Damon smiled as he held his hands up in front of him, showing her his palms. "Fine then. I'm strictly here as a boyfriend and a boyfriend only." Both hands darted forward and pulled her toward him. He leaned in and gently kissed her lips.

Tamira looked away shyly, unable to contain her smile. She'd awakened at some point in the night and couldn't tell if last night was real, or if she dreamed them. In the sleepy fog, her heart broke, longing for the date to be real. She'd cried herself back to sleep, praying for it to be true. His kiss reminded her that it wasn't all just a wonderful dream.

"There does have to be some rules, though." Tamira finally said.

"Rules?" he asked.

"You remember what I am?"

"A glass girl?"

"Yes. Glass breaks. So there must be some unquestionable rules."

"Uh. Okay. Shoot." Damon settled into the couch with a smile.

"Like most other glass-"

"Should I take notes?" Damon interrupted, holding his hand up.

"No. You'll be fine. Just pay attention. First of all-"

His hand shot up again. "Will there be a test?"

Tamira sighed. "No. Now, the main thing that you need to-" She stopped talking and looked at Damon as his hand went into the air yet again. "What?"

"You're very pretty this morning Miss Brannigan."

Tamira smiled, blushing a little. "Thank you."

Damon brushed a loose strand of hair from her face and tucked it behind her ear. "Are you really scared about all this?"

"I am," she admitted. "My poor heart must be ready to just quit. It races when I think about you. It races when I worry about us. It races when I think about going places and doing things I wouldn't do if I didn't have a boyfriend."

"Me too. Look, I need to know exactly what to do so that I won't hurt you. I know you don't want a bodyguard, but I don't want to break you myself doing something stupid." He stood up and paced the room. "I mean, you're right. I'm a goofball. I might accidentally break your arm just messing around. What if I sweep you off your feet in some big romantic gesture and something happens? Huh? What then?"

Tamira smiled. reaching up, she gripped his bicep. "I think it'll be okay."

"What's that supposed to mean?' he asked, flexing his arms.

"Okay, Hercules, settle down. I'm just playing. Anyway, we'll be fine."

"You don't know that. What if our team wins the championship and I high-five you and break your hand off? Have you considered that?"

"Honestly, I can say that I have not considered sporting celebrations. Considering Providence High's track record, though, I think we'll be okay."

He came back to the couch. "Look at me. I'm like a walking accident looking for a home. What were you thinking?"

"I guess I just thought you were cute."

"How cute would I be if I broke your head off during an over exuberant kiss?"

Tamira shook her head, smiling. "Okay. Breathe." She swept her hands upwards as she breathed in, and downwards as she exhaled. She looked at him and smiled. "Better?"

"Some," he admitted. "I am a little tired. I didn't sleep well last night."

"Me either." She took his hand and smiled at him. "It will be okay. I promise."

"How do you do this?" he asked. "How do you not freak out?"

"You do remember that out of everybody in the whole school, I'm the weird girl?"

"They have no idea." Damon shook his head. "Look. I need to know. Just how breakable are you?"

Tamira chewed on her lower lip as she thought. "We are breakable. Very much so, but we're not delicate little things. There just has to be a balance." She slid a hand beneath his and stroked the top with her fingers. "I'm not fragile," she told him. "Well, I am, but fragile like a bomb, not like a flower."

Damon shrugged and smiled at her. "I believe that." He sighed and relaxed into the couch.

"Better?" she asked.

"Some." His eyes narrowed as he looked into hers. "What will break you?"

"Anything that will break glass. A fall, a hard hit by something like a rock or a hammer. Sudden drastic changes in temperature, the right harmonic resonance…"

"Okay," Damon said nodding. "I don't even have a harmonica so we can cross that one off the list."

Tamira laughed, then took his hand again. "You can't be jerking me around a lot, even just playing. No jumping out and scaring me."

Damon's eyes grew wide as he remembered the day on the sidewalk.

Tamira nodded. "Yes. That was huge for me."

"Is that why you had a meltdown?"

Tamira rolled her eyes. "No. I mean it scared the crap out of me and it did put me in danger, risking my very life, but that wasn't what upset me." She looked away. "I had it in my mind to break up with you. I mean, well, you know what I mean."

"Why?"

"Because of this." Tamira waved her hands at herself, then at the entire room. "All this. I just knew that when I told you, you'd freak out and I was going to end it before it got too far along."

"I'm glad my animal magnetism and witty charm changed your mind."

"Me too." She patted his hand, smiling. "I just need *you* to be aware of *you* when you're around *me*. I can take care of myself. I've been doing it a long time. But I've never been this close to a guy. From what I can tell, y'all tend to be…" she waved her hand around while she thought of the right word. "Oafs."

"Oafs?" he asked. "I'm an oaf? Like a big, dumb, clumsy oaf?"

"You just said the same thing about yourself."

"I don't remember saying the word 'oaf.'"

"You're a guy. You're all oafs, but we love y'all despite that," Tamira laughed.

"How are we oafs?"

"Really?" she asked, her brow furrowed. "Boys are always jumping and falling and hitting one another. I mean, you guys hit each other to say hello. Y'all throw stuff at each other. You're always thumping, punching, kicking, tripping each other. Y'all like smashing into each other and laughing about it. Have you ever heard of football?"

Damon shrugged, conceding the point. "Okay. I see what you're saying."

Tamira put a hand to his cheek. "And despite all that here you are, with me on this couch like a normal human being."

Damon took her hand and kissed it. "Your beauty has transformed yon oaf into a prince." He bowed his head, doffing an imaginary hat and extending one hand behind him.

"Look, I know we've been joking around and stuff, but I don't want to downplay this. I've spent my whole life avoiding stuff and being careful."

"My God," Damon looked at her, his eyes wide. "All this time you've been avoiding stuff is because of this. Every day. I mean, to think about the times I bump into somebody, or somebody bumps into me. What a nightmare it must be for you."

Tamira nodded. "Now do you see why I'm so careful?"

"I do." Damon shook his head, thinking. When he looked back at her, the color had drained from his face. "The other day, at the creek. Did you break?"

Tamira shrugged, looking away.

"Did I break you?" Damon asked.

"No," she snapped. "You did not break me." Tamira's eyes searched his face and found the fear she'd been dreading. "You didn't break me."

"But something happened, right?"

"Nothing happened." She stood and walked a few steps away, keeping her back to Damon as she fought back tears. "I am not broken."

Damon joined her, embracing her from behind. He took her hands in his and held them. "I'm sorry."

Tamira spun quickly. Facing him, she put a hand on either side of his face. "Damon Kennedy, I told you I don't need a minder. I don't want you to be afraid every minute of every day. I've done that for years and so has my mother. It's unhealthy and it's just plain miserable."

He shrugged. "Okay. I mean…"

"What? We have to be open about this. I realize it's an incredible thing to have dropped on you."

He nodded in agreement. "I was already worried that something would happen, and I'd screw this up somehow. You know?" He held her fingertips in his and looked down at them. "Now, I can't stop thinking about you being glass and how not to break something."

"I want you to be my boyfriend just like you would be if you didn't know. I only told you because if we're together there have to be parameters. There are just some things I can't do and places I can't go. It's a risk/reward thing. I constantly have to make those decisions. Not you. Not my mother. Me." She pulled his face to her and planted a quick kiss on his lips before releasing him.

"Now. Your concern and worry are adorable and all that right now, but I'm sure it will get old quickly. All I ask is that if I say no, or tell you I can't or won't do something, you respect that and let it go."

"Okay. I think I can do that. There might be a learning curve or something."

"That's fair enough."

"Can I ask you something?" He took her fingers in his.

"Shoot."

"What happens?"

"You mean if I fall or something?"

He nodded, his eyes searching hers.

"If I really fell and just landed on something hard, like concrete, I'd probably shatter."

Damon's mouth fell open and his eyes grew wide. "For real?"

She nodded. "If I got hit hard enough, say in the arm or something, it'd probably break off."

His brow furrowed as he stared at her. "How do you even leave the house?"

"It's a choice."

"You've got to be, like, the bravest person I know. Wow."

Tamira laughed. "Not hardly." She sighed and dropped her gaze. "It doesn't have to be anything big. I can get little chips and stuff too."

"Do you have any?"

Tamira looked at him, reluctant to admit that she did. "Let's talk about something else for a little bit."

He held her hand as she tried to pull away. "It's okay if you do. I mean, I have scars."

Tamira looked over her shoulder at him and sighed. "Yes, I do have a chip. One."

"Can I see it?"

"I'd rather you not."

"Why not?"

"I just don't want you to."

"Okay, that's cool." Damon smiled at her. "It doesn't matter. I mean, I'd show you my scars if you wanted to see them." He let out an exaggerated sigh. "You don't have to share yourself with me. I understand. It's fine."

Her shoulders drooped and she looked at the ceiling with a grunt. "Really?" she asked, shaking her head.

"What?" he asked, laughing.

"Your acting hasn't improved any since yesterday."

"Look, seriously though, you don't have to show me. Really. It's personal. I was wrong to ask."

"Fine. I'll show you, but first, you have to promise me you won't freak out."

"Okay. I won't freak. Is it gruesome?"

"No, it's not gruesome," she replied shaking her head. "It's just a small chip. It's on my hip."

"Your hip?" he asked. His eyes narrowed as he looked at her.

Tamira pulled her shirt up and peeled the waist of her leggings down a few inches, stopping just above the chip. She looked at him, and closed her eyes, not wanting to see his expression. She slid the waistband down to reveal the chip.

Damon bent forward slightly, looking at the small, milky divot on her hip. It was smooth and lighter than her pale skin, like a healed scar, but barely noticeable. He swallowed hard, bending a little closer.

"Can I touch it?"

"No. It's not a dead bird or something."

"When did it happen?"

"The other day." She rolled her pants up and tugged her shirt back down. Tamira looked at the ceiling and whispered, "At the creek."

Damon stood, finding her eyes. "You mean when we..." His voice faded as he spoke. His knees weakened as his mind put the pieces together. She'd gotten chipped when he thoughtlessly rolled onto her, thinking only of kissing her. She was chipped because of him. It was his fault. Damon sank, reaching out a hand to steady himself against the sofa.

Tamira watched the color drain from Damon's face as he realized when and how she'd gotten the chip. He wilted some but caught himself and stayed upright. The truth of who she was, was hitting him hard, but he needed to know. She moved forward and helped him onto the sofa.

"Are you okay?"

Damon nodded. "I'm so sorry. I didn't know."

"That's just it. You didn't know. This isn't your fault."

"But I-"

Tamira held her hand up, stopping him. "No. I told you. We're not going down this road. I am not your responsibility, or your China doll to protect. *I* went with you because *I* wanted to. *I* accepted the risk. *I* got chipped. Not you."

"Okay. Okay. I just want you to know I wouldn't have-"

"Stop. I don't regret it at all. I wish it didn't happen, but it did. There's no making it go away." She took each of his hands in each of hers and looked into his eyes.

"Damon Kennedy, before this chip happened, that was the best day of my whole life. Honestly, I will never forget that day, and not because of the chip. That day was worth far more than a tiny sliver of my hip."

"Still, I'm sorry."

"If I had it to do all over again, knowing this would happen, I'd do it every time." She sighed. "Do you wish I never showed you?"

He shook his head. "No. I'm glad you did."

"I just wanted to make sure you understood exactly what can happen." She ran both hands over her hair, closing her eyes. "I am glass, Damon. I can break. It's a very, very real thing."

Damon nodded, allowing the reality to sink in. "It is. Isn't it?"

"Will you be okay with all this? It's a lot to ask a guy to accept."

"Look, Tamira, I'm not going to say all this isn't blowing my mind. It is. But it hasn't changed anything about the way I feel about you. There's nothing that can do that."

Tamira smiled, wiping a tear from the corner of her eye. "I shouldn't have shown you. I'm so afraid of scaring you away."

"I'm not going anywhere, Tamira."

She looked at him, shaking her head slowly. "It's too much to dump on you at once. I shouldn't have said anything about the chip."

"Of course, you should. It's part of you. It's part of who you are." He took her hand in his. "I like who you are."

She smiled at him. "You're sweet." Tamira dropped her gaze. "I'm sorry."

"For what?" he asked. "You didn't do anything."

"This is a lot to ask a guy to accept. Too much. And I'm not even that pretty."

"Let me decide what is too much for me, okay?" He looked into her eyes and saw a fear that made his heart sink. "You have no idea how amazing you are. Do you? How beautiful?"

"Nothing is amazing about me."

"Oh yeah," he said nodding. "You were amazing before. Now you're like, super amazing. You're one of a kind, Tamira."

"There's actually two of us so…"

"Well, anyway, I'm glad you showed me. I got to see your butt so that was pretty cool."

"You didn't see my butt. *Maybe* the top of my hip."

"I definitely saw some low hip and side butt."

She pushed him playfully. "Why are you such a liar? No butt and maybe the mid hip."

"Nope. There's no going back. You flashed me your butt. I saw it. I mean, it was practically a full moon up in here."

"You're demented. It was the top of my hip," she said laughing. "Nothing else."

"I know what I saw."

"I know what you saw too. And you saw my upper hip."

Damon laughed as he pulled her to him. He leaned in close but paused just short of her lips. "If it matters, it was a very nice side butt."

"Shut up and kiss me, you big oaf."

Chapter Twelve

Damon paced back and forth in front of Tamira's front door. He was eager to see her, but as time for school grew closer, his anxiety was mounting. She didn't want him looking out for her, but how could he not? She was willing to take the risk of going out into the world every day, but he couldn't stop thinking about how easily she'd been chipped.

Tamira opened the door suddenly. "We have a doorbell, weirdo."

Damon stopped and looked at her. Her long hair was pulled up in a ponytail and she was wearing a pair of pink knee-length shorts with a plain white tee shirt. She could have been any regular American girl, but he knew she wasn't.

"Sorry," he said, dropping his gaze.

Her shoulders drooped as she looked at him. He was nervous. "Are you freaking out about school?"

"No," he lied, scanning the lawn.

"Because if you're freaking out, I'm not going to let you walk with me."

"I'm not freaking out."

"You're all sweaty and flustered looking. You look like you're freaking out. I think you're freaking out."

"Well, I'm not," he lied again. "Maybe I sprinted over here. Have you ever thought of that? Just because we're dating now doesn't mean a guy can't keep in shape."

She nodded, smiling. "Yeah, right."

"I'm not playing."

"Sure." She shook her head and laughed. "I've noticed that you've let yourself go these past few days."

"Well, see? There you go."

Tamira stepped out the door and closed it behind her. Looking around, she made sure no one was about before she pushed up to Damon. She pulled him to her and pressed her lips against his. Sliding a hand through his hair to the nape of his neck, she gripped him tightly, holding him to her. She kissed him until her lungs started to burn, then let him go.

"If you start to worry too much, just think about that." Tamira smiled. Damon stared back at her, nodding absently. She laughed and patted him on the chest as she walked past. "You going to school or just hanging around my front door all day like a stalker?"

Damon shook his head, coming back to his senses. He hurried after her, catching up as she neared the steps. This time when she took her time dismounting them to the sidewalk with a deliberate carefulness, he understood why.

"That was quite pleasant," he said, taking her hand.

She nodded. "I thought you might need something to think about today."

"That'll do it." He sighed and ran his free hand through his hair. "Before I forget, my mom wants you to come for supper one night. I guess since I came to your house, she wants you to come to ours. You know since you're my girlfriend and all."

"Okay," Tamira answered casually. "Sounds fun."

"I gotta warn you. My parents are weird."

"Really?" Tamira asked with a laugh. "My mother is glass. Unless your parents are lava, I win the parental weirdness contest."

Damon shrugged his concession. "My folks are always all lovie dovie to each other, though. Even in front of people. It's gross."

"Aww. I think it's sweet."

"But they're old. My dad is like forty."

"What if you were forty, would you still be lovie dovie with me?"

"That's different. You're hot. My mom is, well, my mom."

Tamira laughed, watching Damon out of the corner of her eye. He hastened his pace slightly and swept a few loose stones from the sidewalk with the side of his shoe.

She smiled. It was sweet, for now, so she let it go. She reminded herself that all this was new to him, and she'd promised to be patient. Being a glass girl was probably completely different than dating a glass girl.

Her smile widened as she replayed his words in her mind. "Since you're my girlfriend and all". They were dating. They were an item, a couple. So much had changed, and she couldn't be happier.

"What?" Damon asked, catching her smile.

"Nothing." She rubbed her shoulder against his. "Actually, I was just thinking that for the first time in, well ever, I'm enjoying being me."

Damon took her free hand in his. "I'm enjoying you being you too."

"So," she began, "Are we like, public with all this?"

"I don't see why not unless you're ashamed to be dating me." Damon looked at her, eyebrows raised. "Me being a big oaf and all."

"I think my reputation could withstand it. I mean, You're not like the quarterback team leader person or anything, but you're a solid date."

"Well, I've been thinking. The next time they have tryouts for quarterback team leader person, maybe I'll try out for it."

"Maybe you should."

"Maybe I will."

"Good."

"Good." Damon laughed. "How did I get so lucky?" He leaned over, rubbing their shoulders together as they walked.

"I was just wondering the same thing."

"Dude. Where have you been?"

Damon watched Brady slide into the seat beside him. "Around."

"I texted you Friday night like fifty times. We had an epic Black Ops tourney. Man, you missed it. I was on fire."

"I was busy."

A dirty grin slid across Brady's lips. "That's what the word is. I heard you had a date with Tamira Brannigan."

Damon sat up in his chair. "So?"

"Nothing man, just saying. Don't get all swole on me."

Damon looked at Brady for another moment, then turned to the front of the class. "I did have a date with her."

"You get anywhere?" Brady asked in a whisper.

Damon rolled his eyes. "I wouldn't tell you if I did."

"Oh man, you dog you. You did. How far you get?"

"Dude, you really need to chill. I didn't say I got anywhere. You did. I had supper at her house with Tamira and her mother."

"They said you two showed up holding hands this morning. Y'all a thing now?"

"Are you the school reporter all of a sudden? Dude, this isn't middle school."

"What do you see in that weirdo?"

"How about you shut your stinking mouth?" Damon asked. His words were sharper and louder than he expected, drawing the attention of the surrounding students.

"How about you calming down?"

"How about I punch you in your big mouth?" Damon stared at Brady until he turned in his seat and faced the front of the class. Brady relaxed into his seat as the teacher called the class to order. When Damon spared him another glance, Brady gave him another dirty grin and a thumbs up. Damon sighed and shook his head.

"You're an idiot. Why don't you just-"

"Mister Kennedy, do you have something to share?"

Damon's cheeks flushed as everyone in the class turned to look at him. "No ma'am, I don't. I'm sorry."

"Very well then," the teacher continued. "Now that Mister Kennedy has finished interrupting, let's all take out our textbooks and turn to chapter three."

Damon took a deep breath to calm the anger rising in his chest. Stupid Brady, he thought. Why can't people just leave things alone?

When Tamira slid into the seat across the table from him, Damon felt the frustration that had been building since first period begin to fade. He looked at her and smiled. "Hi there beautiful."

"Hey. How'd your morning go?"

Damon shrugged. "Okay, I guess."

"Walking up it looked like you were deep in thought. Care to share?"

"It was nothing," he lied. "Guess I was just spacing."

Tamira reached across the table and put a hand on his. "It'll be okay." She smiled when his eyes found hers, but it faded when his eyes diverted to something behind her. She looked over her shoulder. A group of kids sitting at the next table were staring at them and whispering among themselves.

Tamira turned back to Damon with a sigh. She patted his hand. "Don't sweat it, Damon. They're not worth the time. Trust me. It's a losing battle."

Damon shook his head and turned his attention back to her. He smiled again, his anger falling. "I just wish it could be us. People are jerks."

Tamira nodded as she drank from the glass of apple juice. "News Flash, I'm the weird girl. It's just one more reason for you to not like me. You were warned."

"Stop. I don't give a crap what these idiots think. They don't even know you. They'd like you if they knew you."

"Well, things are what they are." Tamira shrugged. She watched Damon's eyes dart back to the table behind her. "You don't have to sit with me, you know. It's okay."

"No, it's not. That's crazy. You're my girlfriend. I should sit with you. I want to sit with you." He caressed her hand.

"Then chill out and let things be what they are. It's going to drive you crazy if you let it." She leaned over the table. "People don't dislike me because of who I am or who I'm not. They think I'm weird because of the way I have to react to being what I am. I'm different. Now, my secret is our secret. You know how this school thing is. People are immature and mean. There's nothing we can do about either one."

"It's just stupid."

She nodded. "I guess it is. It's always been that way and probably always will be. You crossed a line, Damon. Popular guys don't usually date weird girls."

"You're not weird."

Tamira laughed and shrugged. "Look around. There seems to be a consensus that says otherwise."

"I hate them for being this way toward you. They don't have a clue how awesome you are, how brave you are. They can't even see how beautiful you are."

"To be fair, I didn't really do much to change that last part. I never had a reason to care what I looked like. Until now. Nobody ever noticed me, so I just kept it plain and comfortable, you know."

"I saw how beautiful you are the first time I saw you."

She smiled. "Well, Damon Kennedy, you're an exceptional human being."

"So are you."

Tamira shook her head. "I'm just the weird girl."

"No, you're not. Stop saying that. You're beautiful and amazing and it's time everyone knew it."

"What are you doing?" she asked, watching him swipe their trays aside. "No. Do not make a scene. Damon." Her pleas fell on deaf ears as he climbed atop the lunch table.

Most of the chatter died as soon as Damon stepped onto the table, the rest faded as everyone else began to notice him. The entire lunchroom fell silent when he started talking.

"Hey, everyone, some of you may know me, some don't. I'm kinda new here. But my name is Damon Kennedy and I just wanted everyone to know that I am dating a beautiful, amazing girl named Tamira Brannigan." Damon scanned the room as people began to whisper among themselves. "Most of you know her. What you don't know is what a smart, generous, and kind, amazingly beautiful girl she is."

Tamira shrank at the table, hiding her face behind her hand.

"I have heard a few people whispering and I've seen your stares and I want you to know I don't care one bit. Look all you want. She's amazing and beautiful-"

Someone in the back yelled out, "You already said that." A low rumble of laughter swept through the room.

"Well, I'm saying it again. She is beautiful. And if anyone in this school has a problem with us dating, or has some snarky comment, stand up now and we'll discuss it man to man."

Damon's heart sank when a hulking boy a few tables over began to stir. He stood and slowly turned to face him, his massive arms stretching the sleeves of his tee-shirt. He tossed his hands up, throwing a nod at Damon.

"Not you, big fella," Damon replied, pointing at him. "If anyone but this hugely muscled gentleman, or really anybody half his size or smaller has a problem-" Waiting for the laughter to die down, he gave the big guy a thumbs up as he sat back down.

Tamira tugged at the legs of his jeans. "The teachers are coming."

"You come to see me. I'm proud to be dating her so if you got a problem with it, you can just piss off." Damon jumped from the table to a smattering of applause as the trio of male teachers surrounded him.

"Okay, Romeo, come with us."

Damon slipped between them and grabbed Tamira's hand. "Parting is such sweet sorrow." He planted a kiss on the back of her hand as two of the men hauled him away. "I have only just begun to date," he yelled over his shoulder as they ushered him between the tables. The lunchroom erupted in laughter.

People began to stand and applaud as he passed, hurried along by a teacher on each arm. Tamira shook her head as she watched the spectacle, both overjoyed and mortified at the same time.

A smile came to her lips as she hid behind her hand. Dam you, Damon Kennedy, she thought. Why'd you have to be the best boyfriend in the world?

"Oh look, here she is." A snarl crawled across the face of Rachel Parson as she watched Tamira navigate her way down the hallway toward them.

"What does he see in her?" Brittany Booth asked, shaking her head. "She's so... plain."

"Maybe all they have is ugly girls up in Indiana. Must be all the corn." Rachel looked at the poster on the wall between them and smiled. "Come on." She tore the poster down and moved to meet Tamira.

Tamira stopped when the girls stepped in front of her. She drew in a calming breath and looked up with a forced smile. "Hello, ladies."

"Aren't you Tamira Brannigan?" Rachel asked, putting a hand on the curve of her hip. She was filled out more than most of the girls, especially in the places that got boys' attention.

"I am," Tamira answered. Rachel knew who she was, and they both knew it.

"The whole school is talking about Damon Kennedy and his lunchroom theatrics."

Tamira smiled, then shrugged. She could never get into a fight with these girls or anyone, but she didn't like them. They were mean and petty and until now she'd managed to escape the brunt of their attention.

"Personally, I'd have been mortified with such a public display of affection." Rachel flipped her long hair over her shoulder as she stared at Tamira.

"Yeah, it sounds like something desperate to me," Brittany added.

"But Brit, he must be desperate." They both scanned Tamira from head to toe then started laughing.

"Okay ladies, are we done here? Because I need to get to class. Not everybody can hope to grow up to be some guy's trophy wife."

Rachel put her arm on the wall, blocking Tamira as she tried to pass. "So," she began, holding up the poster. "Does all this big production mean you're finally going to get asked to a dance, Tamira?"

Tamira's eyes washed over the poster advertising the homecoming dance and widened involuntarily with excitement. She dropped her gaze, but it was too late. They'd seen her reaction.

"You'll need a dress, Cinderella," Brittany laughed, eyeing Tamira's clothes.

"And some make-up," Rachel added. "Maybe a lot of make-up." The two girls shared a laugh as they pushed past her.

"Oh," Brittany said, turning back around, "We're in high school now. If a boy brings you to a dance, he's going to want something. You better be prepared to put out."

"As if," Rachel added.

The girls exploded in laughter as they turned and walked away. Tamira sighed and shook her head. The more things change, she thought, the more they stay the same.

"You're lucky you only got two days of detention." Tamira looked at Damon as they walked home. "You're a freaking nutcase."

"I just told them what was up. Maybe Assistant Principal Perkins is a hopeless romantic."

Tamira laughed. "You don't know him. He's anything but a hopeless romantic. A sadist, maybe."

"Maybe he knew he couldn't stand in the way of true love."

"Maybe he thought you were from the Special Ed class," Tamira laughed. "I'm beginning to wonder myself. The whole school is talking about what you did."

"So?" Damon said with a casual shrug.

"So? People are looking at me now."

"I thought you didn't care what people thought about you."

"I don't care what people think, but that's not what I said."

"That's what it sounded like."

Tamira stopped. She rubbed her forehead then pushed a hand over her hair. "I said people are looking at me."

"They should be looking at you, you're very pretty, Tamira."

She opened her mouth to speak but just shook her head. "I don't…" Her words faded as she started walking again.

"What's wrong?" he asked, catching up with her. "Did I embarrass you?"

"No. Well yes, but in a good way." She sidestepped a discarded soda can and rejoined him. "Before, it was easy to just sneak into school and sneak out. I was just there, like a light fixture. Nobody ever paid me any attention. I mean, even the mean girls didn't even bother messing with me."

Damon bent forward, looking at her face as they walked. "Is that what you wanted?"

Tamira shrugged. "It was easier."

"But was that what you wanted?"

"It never mattered what I wanted before," she spat, her words stronger than she'd intended.

Damon's shoulders drooped and a wave of sadness washed over his face. "Tamira Brannigan, it matters what you want now. You better get used to it because as long as you'll let me be in your life, it's always going to matter what you want." He put an arm across her shoulders and pulled her to him.

"I'm freaking terrified now. Thanks a lot."

"Well, you didn't have to fall in love with me. You could have resisted my devilish good looks and clever repartee."

"Yeah, right," she said shaking her head.

"You're probably right," he said nodding. "Who am I kidding? You never stood a chance."

She laughed, elbowing him in the ribs playfully. "It was a little embarrassing, but it was sweet."

"I couldn't help myself. Something just came over me."

"That seems to be happening a lot lately. Maybe you should see a doctor."

"I'm simply a man-" he looked at her with an eyebrow arched- "overcome by desire."

"No," Tamira said, stepping away from him. "Do not kiss me."

"Oh, I'm gonna kiss you."

"You're not overcome with desire, you're just crazy."

Damon grabbed her hands and pulled her to the edge of the shrubs that lined her yard. "Tamira Brannigan, I am crazy about you, and I want the world to know it."

Tamira's eyes searched his face. "I've never met anyone like you."

Damon smiled. "I've never met anyone like you either."

"Well, duh," she laughed. "I'm a glass girl, so that's probably true."

Damon put the back of his hand to his forehead. "I'm feeling overcome right now."

"I think it's just the heat. You'll be okay. Maybe a cold shower will help."

"No. I'm definitely feeling overcome with something. What could it be?" he asked, stroking his chin. He snapped his fingers. "Desire, that's right. I'm overcome with desire."

Tamira laughed as he pulled her to him and sank behind the shrubs. When he pushed his lips to hers, her body relaxed as all the day's worries melted away. Every day she was with him became the best day of her life and she couldn't wait to see what tomorrow would bring.

Chapter Thirteen

"Detention?"

Damon dropped his head, not wanting to see his mother's face.

"For jumping on the lunchroom table and cursing? What has come over you, Damon?" She shook the detention slip at him. "Detention?"

"Can I at least tell my side of the story?" he asked.

"How could you possibly rationalize this type of behavior?"

"Can I explain?"

"Oh yes. You better start doing some explaining."

"Okay, so people were all whispering and stuff about me dating Tamira and-"

"Dating? The girl you had dinner with on Friday?"

"Yes."

"I thought you just met her."

"I did, but we've been talking and stuff in school." He watched his mother roll her eyes and realized that he was fighting an uphill battle.

"And you two are 'dating' already?" She used her fingers to make air quotes.

"Yes," he sighed.

"Don't you think it's awful quick?"

"No." Damon rubbed his face with both hands. "Anyway, she's not one of the popular kids so people are whispering and talking about us."

"Why are they whispering? Are you one of the popular kids?" she asked, a hopeful smile tugging at the corners of her mouth.

Damon answered with a shrug, but his mother's smile widened. If it helped his case, he wasn't going to argue the point.

"So, I really like this girl, Tamira. She's smart and funny and pretty."

Damon watched his mother's face soften. "You're smitten aren't you."

"If that means I like her, then yes. I guess so." Damon propped his elbow on the table and rubbed his forehead. "So anyway, I don't know what happened. One minute I was seeing people staring at us while we were eating lunch, then the next thing I knew I was on the table proclaiming my feelings and challenging anybody who didn't like it."

She smiled, nodding her head slowly. "I'll say this. It was a very romantic gesture. I'm sure she appreciated it."

"She said I embarrassed her to death."

"She said that, but I'm sure deep down she loved it. You standing up for her and proclaiming your love to the whole school. That was very brave."

"I said feelings," Damon corrected. "Not love."

She threw a dismissive wave at him. "Whatever. It's very sweet and noble of you, but you can't be leaping onto tables, son. You can't change the world, Damon. You're not Don Quixote."

"Who's that?"

She shook her head. "Don't worry about it. At least you're handsome."

"Mom," he protested.

"The point is, I don't want anything like this to ever happen again. This is your one get out of jail free card for the whole school year. You better be on your toes from here on out. You hear me?"

"I hear you, mom. I'm sorry. It won't happen again. I promise."

Her smile faded as she watched her son's face grow serious. "Everything okay?"

Damon shrugged. "Yeah. I guess."

"You look like you got a gut punch."

Damon shook his head. "She's different, mom."

"Different? How so?"

Damon sighed. He couldn't tell her Tamira's secret, but he wanted some advice. "She's just not like any other girl I ever met."

"Is that a good thing?"

"It is, I think. I mean, it doesn't bother me."

"Damon, look, if you like her, it shouldn't matter if she's different, or not so popular or whatever."

"It doesn't bother me. I just…" He sighed. "I don't know."

"I know it's tough. You've got a lot of stuff running through your head, and probably your heart right now." She smiled at her son. "You just do the best you can, treat her good, and be a gentleman. Everything else will work out."

Damon smiled. "I hope so."

She smiled, thumbing the edge of the detention slip. "I guess my little boy is growing up." She shook her head and wadded the paper in her fist. "I'm not going to bother your dad with this. Don't make me regret it."

"I won't, Mom. I promise." He got up and threw his arms around her shoulders. "Thank you, mom. You're the best."

"Yeah, yeah. There better not be a next time. I mean it."

"There won't be." Damon lingered in his embrace. "I love you, mom."

She smiled and reached back, mussing his hair. "I love you too, my little Romeo."

"I thought you said I was Don Coyote."

She laughed. "Don Quixote. Key-o-tee. Never mind. Just take care of your hair. You've got a gorgeous head of hair. That'll help."

"Thanks, Mom."

"Well, don't think you're off the hook, mister. I fully expect you to do more around here for the rest of the week."

"Aw, man. C'mon, mom."

"You can walk Tamira home, but I expect you back here right after."

"Fine then," Damon relented. He was getting off light and he knew it. Still, not being able to hang out with Tamira was going to make it a long week.

Damon scooped a handful of wet, rotting leaves from the gutter and dropped it into the bucket hanging on his ladder with a grunt of disgust. Monday had brought detention immediately after school, followed by mowing the lawn when he got home. Tuesday was detention again and gutter cleaning.

"Hey, kid."

Damon looked around. The voice was deep and throaty, like a man's. From this vantage point, he could see the sidewalk, but it was deserted. He shook his head, assuming it was a neighbor talking to someone else. He scooped more leaves out of the gutter and dropped them into the bucket.

"Hey, kid."

Damon continued his work, deciding that it was probably one of his friends trying to be funny. He wanted to finish as quickly as possible so he could call Tamira.

"Are you feeling overcome with anything?"

A smile swept across his face as he turned, recognizing the voice. Tamira stepped from behind one of the shrubs and waved at him.

Damon looked around for his parents. When he didn't see them, he hurried down the ladder and went to Tamira.

"You poor thing," she said, offering him a sad smile. "I'm sorry."

"Me too." Tamira was beyond the short fence on the outside of the shrubs. "I feel like it's been forever since I saw you." He reached between the bushes and took her hand.

"You saw me at lunch," she reminded him with a smile.

"I know, but we couldn't sit together and hold hands like we do on your couch."

"I know. I miss that. Just a few more days."

Damon looked around. "Come down here to the end of the fence. A bush died and I can get closer to you."

He released her hand and went to the back of the yard. Pushing past the last evergreen, he leaned on the fence.

"I don't want you to get in more trouble because of me," Tamira said as she joined him.

Damon leaned over the fence and reached for her, but she recoiled.

"Your hands." She leaned in when he withdrew his grimy hands, delivering a long kiss.

"I can't stand not being able to touch you."

"I know. Me too." Tamira caressed his cheek. "This is kinda fun though. It's like I'm visiting you in prison or something."

"I feel like I'm in prison. Stupid detention."

Tamira gave him a sad smile, extending her hands over the fence.

"I'm filthy," he said, showing her his dirty palms.

"I don't care. I'll take you any way I find you." She took his hands when he reached over the fence. "Friday will be here before you know it. Then we can be together more. All weekend."

"It can't come soon enough for me." Damon leaned in, putting his forehead against hers. "I know it sounds corny, but I miss you."

"I was thinking the same thing. If it counts for anything, you scored some major brownie points with my mom with the whole lunchroom thing."

"Yay me. How about you?"

Tamira raised her head, looking at him. "Big time brownie points. Many, many points." She planted a quick kiss on his lips. "I can't stay long. Mom didn't want me to come as it was. I just wanted to see you."

"Just a little bit longer," he pleaded. "I've been stuck doing this junk and all I can think about is you."

"I know, walking home from school alone already feels weird. Today I was thinking about how I used to do it every day and it made me sad a little bit. I was just moving from one place to another, you know. I was alone at school and alone at home. It was just a change of scenery."

"I wish I'd grown up here. We could have been together for years by now."

"Not hardly. If you'd grown up here, you'd probably be like Easton and that bunch. You wouldn't even realize I was there."

Damon shook his head. "I don't think so." He reached out and touched her cheek. "I couldn't imagine not noticing you."

Tamira leaned into his hand, forgetting about the dirt. "I'm glad you did."

"Me too." Damon's eyes drifted to the thumb stroking her cheek and his eyes widened.

Tamira closed her eyes and sighed, her shoulders falling. "There's dirt on my face now isn't there?"

"No," he lied, hiding a smile. "Not at all." He wiped his hand on his pants and showed her. "See, nothing."

Tamira shook her head. "Am I supposed to just walk home with a dirty face now?"

"You could stay here with a dirty face. I don't mind."

Tamira ran her fingertips across her cheek and looked at them, gasping at the black grime. "It really is dirty."

Damon used his remaining dirty hand to wipe her cheek, smearing more grime on it. "Oops," he said grinning.

"Damon Kennedy," she sighed. "You've had it now." Using one finger, she wiped the dirt from her cheek and smeared it on his nose.

Damon gasped, feigning offense. "Oh, it's on now, girlie."

Tamira stepped back out of his reach. "Come and get me, jailbird."

"Oh, I'll come and get you." Damon started over the fence but stopped when his mother called him. "It's your lucky day," he said, grinning. He hurried around the shrub and back into his yard. "Yeah, mom."

"What are you doing over there?"

"I, uh, saw a bird nest in here yesterday. I was just checking on it."

"What's on your face?" she asked.

"I was cleaning the gutters, remember?"

"Yeah," she said, eyeing him suspiciously. "Maybe you should get back to it. Supper will be ready soon."

"Okay. Just a second." Damon ducked back behind the bush. "I gotta go."

Tamira leaned in, offering the cheek he'd smeared with grime.

"Really?" he asked. "Fine then. It's better than nothing." As he leaned in to kiss her, Tamira turned her head, meeting his lips with hers.

"Go," she said smiling. "Call me later."

Damon smiled. "You know I will."

Tamira watched him push back around the shrub and disappear. She lingered long enough for him to climb the ladder. She offered a wave and blew him a kiss before leaving.

Walking home, lost in thought, Tamira marveled at how much her life had changed in the past few weeks. Damon had entered her life unexpectedly, completely out of the blue. The morning of the first day of school, she'd dreaded another year of being teased or even worse, being ignored. She hadn't dared to dream something like Damon Kennedy would happen to her.

She allowed her eyes to drift across the two-lane road to the other sidewalk. How many times had she walked that very sidewalk alone, fighting tears and loneliness? Hundreds? Thousands? Twice a day, every day for the entire school year. The middle school was two blocks beyond the high school and the elementary school just around the corner from it. Her path had been the same for years, now she didn't have to walk it by herself.

So many times, she'd walked alone, telling herself that things were fine, lying to herself that things would be better tomorrow. She never asked to be a glass girl. It was thrust upon her by some strange magic by a man she never met. He'd sentenced her to a life of being different; of being alone.

"Until now," she whispered, and a smile crept to her lips. The sidewalk hadn't changed, but she had. Like Pinocchio, she thought. She'd been brought to life. She was alive now. The weight that used to be her heart had awakened and it was all because of Damon.

She turned, ambling into the crosswalk, smiling as she thought about the look in his eyes. The screeching of tires yanked her from her thoughts. She looked around wide-eyed as the car came to a stop three feet from her. The man inside waved his hands wildly, giving her a piece of his mind.

Tamira gasped, her hand going to her chest. "I'm sorry," she said, waving as she hurried across the street. She shook her head, watching as the car moved on.

She rubbed her forehead, collecting herself. If the car had hit her, she'd be dead now, shattered into a thousand pieces.

She drew in a deep breath and blew it out slowly as a shudder ran through her. Some things had changed drastically, but many things were the same as they'd always been. She'd been careless and it almost got her killed. She couldn't let it happen again.

Chapter Fourteen

Crystal Brannigan threw the front door of her house open and rushed out, wrapping Damon in a tight embrace. "You precious, sweet, sweet, wonderful thing you."

Damon froze, not knowing what else to do. He didn't know why Tamira's mom was hugging him. It wasn't unpleasant, but a little awkward.

She broke the embrace and held him at arms-length, looking at him with misty eyes. "I've been telling myself all week that I wouldn't do that. I'm sorry if I made you feel uncomfortable."

"It's okay," he said. "I guess."

"Tamira told me all about what you did in school on Monday." She patted his cheek then folded her hands to her chest. "So romantic and sweet."

"Oh." Damon nodded. With his detention and the extra chores, he hadn't seen her all week. "It's nothing really."

"Yes, it is. It's huge. You're my hero."

"I don't know about all that. It's not like I planned it or anything. It just happened." He sighed. "Anyway, I got detention."

"A small price to pay, kiddo," she said ushering him inside. "A small price to pay."

He was about to tell her he'd also had to "volunteer" to help his dad around the house as well when he saw

Tamira. She was standing on the bottom step, smiling as her mother delivered Damon to her.

"You two have fun. Are you sure you don't want me to call you a cab?"

"No, ma'am. It's only a few blocks."

"We can walk, Mama."

"Okay. Call me when you're ready to come home and I'll send a cab."

"I will."

Crystal put a hand to her chest as she watched Damon offer his hand and lead Tamira down the steps. When he slid his arm behind her, putting a hand on the small of her back, she shot Tamira a wink.

"Have fun you two." Standing in the doorway, she watched them walk down the sidewalk holding hands. She smiled and sighed deeply. All the worry about Tamira spending her life alone vanished. No matter how long things lasted with this boy, she'd always have this time to look back on. First boyfriends went a long way to helping a young woman learn what they wanted in a man, and this one was setting the bar high.

"I'm sorry about all that." Tamira swung their hands playfully. "She's been weepy and emotional all week."

"Parents are weird like that. My mom keeps calling me Don Keytote or something."

"Don Quixote?" Tamira asked.

"Damon threw his free hand into the air. "What? Does everybody know this guy?"

"Everybody but you, apparently." Tamira cocked an eyebrow playfully as she looked at him.

"Funny. You should be a comedian."

"I'm playing," she said, nudging him with her shoulder. "You should look it up."

Damon shook his head. "It's not that important."

"Do you want to know who he was?"

"I feel like I should say yes, so yes." Damon moved around Tamira, putting himself between her and the street.

"He lived in the old days. He was a nobleman who read so many books about chivalry and romance that he lost his mind. He got a lance, or maybe a sword, I don't remember. Anyway, he went around fighting lost causes, trying to make the world a better place."

Damon scratched his chin, thinking. "Sounds a lot like me now that you mention it."

"I agree," she said laughing. "He was a nut too."

"And the comedian is back."

Tamira leaned over and kissed his cheek. "If you're a nut, you're my nut and I wouldn't have you any other way."

Damon pulled her to the edge of the sidewalk and threw his arms around her. He hugged her tightly, holding her to him. When he released her, he took her hands in his.

"This week has felt like a month."

Tamira smiled, nodding in agreement. "I feel like I've missed you."

"Me too. It's sucked not being able to touch you."

Damon turned, holding her hand as they started walking again. "Are you nervous about meeting my folks?"

She shrugged. "Some, I guess. I want them to like me."

"How could they not?"

Tamira shrugged. "I'm not exactly a social butterfly if you haven't noticed."

Damon shook his head. "What? That's news to me. I never noticed a thing."

She slapped him on the chest playfully. "I know how I am. I didn't make it that way. It just sort of happened."

"No one could blame you. I'd be a nervous wreck. If I were your mom, I wouldn't let you leave the house."

"She tried. That's exactly what she wanted."

"I'm glad she didn't hide you. We might not have ever met."

"I know." Tamira squeezed his hand. "Do you ever think about that?" she asked. "Just how crazy all of this is?"

"Us?" he asked, nodding. "I was lying in bed the other night, you know, not studying classic literature, and thinking how things just sort of came together for us." He nudged her further away from the street as a delivery truck approached. "Like, how I just happened to be standing there when you came to school. Five minutes later or earlier and I would have missed you altogether."

"I know. It's crazy," she agreed. "I mean, my mother is some crazy, supernatural creation wrought from agony and despair by a man who loved her so much that he didn't want to live if she couldn't be in his life. Could you imagine that?"

Damon smiled and squeezed her hand but said nothing.

"They said Pop Pop died of exhaustion, but I think he poured everything thing he had into that baby to save her. Through some sort of magic of pure love and fire and heat, he poured his life force into a perfect glass figurine and made her real."

"That's so amazing. I mean, it still sounds crazy, but amazing too. Know what I'm saying? I mean, it doesn't even sound possible, yet here you are." He squeezed her hand. "And here we are."

"I know." Tamira shook her head. "And then my mom had me and I was just like her."

"Why do you think that happened that way? I mean, shouldn't you have been half human, or regular, or whatever you want to call it?"

"You'd think that. Mom said she was surprised when I came out the way I did." Tamira sighed and squeezed his hand. "Mama always just said it was because of Pop Pop." She shrugged. "That's all she ever says when I ask questions. 'Don't question the magic'."

"It's wild." He stopped and looked at her. "There's just one of you, and I meet it." His eyes searched hers. "I mean, stuff like that doesn't just happen."

Tamira nodded as they started walking again. "You know, for a long time, my mom kept me at home and taught me. I didn't go to school until fifth grade. I was scared all the time back then, but I didn't want to hide anymore. Even as young as I was, I knew I had to get out in the world, as dangerous as it was. For years I didn't have any real friends. No boyfriends."

She squeezed Damon's hand. "But I knew I was this way for a reason. I just kept telling myself that over and over. Whatever magic made my mother, and eventually me, didn't do that so I could hide from the world. I had a purpose."

"That makes sense. And you were right. Maybe that's why my dad took this job. He wasn't even looking for another job. One day a friend just called and told him about it. It was more money, so he applied. Inside of a week, they called and offered him the job. We moved here as soon as the school year was over."

"See. It's kismet. All the forces in the universe got together and made these roads and made them intersect at a particular place and time. Then they took a boy from Indiana and a girl from Providence, Alabama and put them on these roads and just sat back and watched."

"A glass girl from Providence, Alabama," he added.

She dropped her gaze to the sidewalk. "Did you never consider just running away when I told you?"

"You know the weird part is that I didn't. Honestly, the thought never even crossed my mind. Not even for a second." He kicked a rock down the sidewalk, watching it go.

"I'm glad you stayed."

Damon stopped walking and turned to her. He took her hands in his. "I can't pretend to know how or why we met when we did. I can't even explain why I felt the way I did when I saw you. I mean, I don't even understand what you are and how you got that way. All I can say is that we're here, right now and I feel like the luckiest guy in the world."

Tamira hugged him, laying her head on his chest. "I love you, Damon Kennedy."

"I love you too, Tamira Brannigan. I just hope you still love me after you meet my folks." He turned and looked at the house behind him. "This is me."

Tamira's mouth fell open. When she'd visited earlier in the week, she didn't that it was the same house. Her attention was on Damon, and she'd seen the plain, simple back of the house. The house before her was a massive anti-bellum structure with a front porch that went from a high turret on the left to a two-story wall on the other side of the house. In the gables, its white clapboards gave way to decorative siding that she always thought looked like rows of fish scales. She'd always imagined living in it would be like living in a castle.

"Are you okay?" he asked, taking her by the elbow.

"Uh-huh," she said, her anxiety rising.

"It's just a house. To be honest it's drafty. You'll see. My dad complains about the electricity bill every month."

"Uh-huh," she said again, allowing herself to be led up the sidewalk.

"If you don't want to do this, you don't have to."

Tamira shook her head, collecting herself. "I'm fine. I just always thought this was a beautiful house. When I was a kid, I used to fantasize about living here."

"Sometimes dreams come true," he said with a coy smile. "I know mine did."

"Stop," she laughed as they climbed the steps. "Let's go inside. I think the heat's getting to you."

"Wait." Damon stopped short of the front door and took her by the shoulders, turning her to face him. "There's something I have to tell you before we go inside."

"What?" she asked, her eyes wide. "Don't you drop a bomb on me on the doorstep, Damon Kennedy."

"It's not anything like that. I just wanted to tell you that I'm feeling like I might be getting-"

"Don't say it," she said, laughing as she put a finger to his lips. "You'll have me all flustered when I meet your parents. My face will be all red and splotchy."

"I'm obercumb whiff desire," he said around her finger.

"No," she said, pushing him back playfully. Damon slid his hands around her hips and pulled her closer, but before he could lean in for the kiss Tamira reached out and rang the doorbell.

Damon froze when the door opened.

His mother stared at them; her brow furrowed inquisitively. "Damon?"

He released Tamira and stepped back.

"Why'd you ring the bell?" she asked, eyeing him suspiciously.

He shot Tamira a smile then shrugged. "I didn't mean to."

"You must be Tamira," she said, stepping onto the porch between them. Damon moved out of the way as his mother put an arm around Tamira's shoulders and ushered her inside.

"I'm here too, mom."

"I know," she said over her shoulder. "Come in and close the door. Your dad will have a fit about the air conditioner as it is."

Damon shook his head as he watched them disappear into the house. "Well played," he said with a grin.

Damon looked across the table at Tamira. When she caught his eye, he shot her a wink. She smiled and dropped her gaze to her plate. She pushed the piece of swordfish around then put the uneaten stalks of asparagus in its place. So far, the conversation had been light and airy, but her nerves hadn't calmed yet.

"Not a big fish eater?"

Tamira looked up and found Damon's dad looking at her, his eyebrows raised inquisitively. He was a tall man with a deep, authoritative voice He was attractive, like Damon, but his hair had already begun thinning.

"Oh, uh, Yessir. I like it. It's delicious." She forked a piece off the slab on her plate and ate it with a smile.

"Do you and Damon have many classes together?" his mother asked, changing the subject.

"No ma'am. Just math really, and lunch period." Damon's head shot up. He stared at her wide-eyed, then looked at his mother.

She smiled. "Yes, lunch. I always remember that as a very active time when I was in school. Giving kids a chance to socialize freely and express themselves."

Tamira watched Damon give his mother a pleading look, then stole a glance at his dad. He was busy sawing a piece of asparagus. He hadn't heard a word.

"How do you feel about lunch period, Tamira?"

Tamira nodded, fighting a smile as she watched Damon's tortured expression deepen. "I love it. I'm a big fan of self-expression. Spontaneous expressions, passionate expressions. Really anything along those lines is pretty cool." When Damon's eyes begged her to stop, she dropped her eyes to her plate, fighting a smile. "But Literature is my favorite."

Damon's mother sniggered.

His father looked up and laughed. "You'll be good for this one then. The only things he reads are text messages and cereal boxes."

Tamira fought to restrain her laughter.

"Good one, Dad. Thanks." Damon gave him a thumbs up. "Just super."

"What?" he asked laughing. "Am I wrong?"

"Actually, Mister Kennedy," Tamira began, coming to Damon's defense. "We were discussing Don Quixote on the way over here."

"That's the guy who boxed windmills, right?"

"Close enough dear," his wife said. She smiled at Damon, offering a reprieve. "Why don't we let these two have some time to talk while we have a drink in the den."

"Sounds good to me." Damon's father stabbed a chunk of fish and put it in his mouth as he stood. "Tamira, it was a pleasure meeting you. Please, feel free to come again."

"Yes, Tamira, it's been lovely meeting you. Thank you for coming."

"Yes ma'am. Thanks for inviting me."

"I mean it. Please don't be a stranger." She mussed Damon's hair as she passed his chair.

Damon waited until his parents were clear of the room before grunting. "I told you they were weird."

"They seem nice." Tamira wiped the corners of her mouth and laid the cloth napkin over her plate.

"That was brutal, and you were no help."

Tamira laughed. "I'm sorry. I was just trying to get on your mom's good side. Besides, that's what you get for putting gook on my face the other day."

"Oh, who is in cahoots with who's mom now?"

"I'm sorry," she replied, still laughing.

"And the meal. Geesh. We never eat swordfish unless we're at the beach." Damon shook his head. "I told you they were goofy."

"It's fine, really. It was good."

"You didn't eat much."

Tamira looked down at her plate, then at him. She crinkled her nose. "Don't tell your mom this, but I hate asparagus and that might be the first bite of fish I've eaten in ten years. Not a fan."

"See." Damon got up and came to her side of the table. "Let's go look in the kitchen for some real food."

Chapter Fifteen

Tamira knocked quietly on her mother's bedroom, then opened it a crack. "You up?"

"Sweetie, I didn't even hear you come in." She closed her book and laid it on the nightstand. "I completely lost track of the time. Sorry I didn't get to thank Damon for walking you home."

Tamira waved her off casually. "He couldn't stay. He had to get back." She leaned against the door casing with a sigh, resting her head on the wood."

Crystal looked at her daughter's face and smiled. The soft light from the bedside lamp reflected off her break on her cheek and danced on the walls.

"Come," she said, folding the covers back on the empty side of the bed. "Lay with Mama and tell me about your night."

Tamira hurried across the room and jumped into the bed. She pulled the covers to her chin and settled into the pillows, looking at her mother.

"Is it supposed to be like this?"

"Love?" Crystal asked with a smile.

Tamira nodded, fighting back a flood of emotions.

Crystal slid down in the bed and put an arm around Tamira. "If you're lucky it does."

"I've never felt like I was going to throw up so many times in my life, but in a good way."

Crystal smiled. "That's the good stuff, Tamira. When they said love hurts, they weren't kidding."

"Mama, he says these things that are just…" she shook her head and wiped a tear from her cheek. She accepted the tissues from her mother and clutched them in her fist. "I mean, he tells me I'm beautiful and I look in his eyes and I can see he means it. And he makes me believe it."

"You are beautiful, Tamira." Crystal brushed the hair from her daughter's face with a smile. Her new regiment was already paying dividends, resulting in a fuller, more vibrant crop of auburn hair.

She shrugged. "I asked him if he ever considered running away when I told him what we were. He said it never crossed his mind to leave."

"Do you believe him?"

Tamira nodded. "I do." A wave of tears washed over her cheeks. "I just love him so much, Mama."

"I know you do, sweetie. He's a really nice boy."

Tamira wiped her face and looked at her mother. "You know what's scarier than that? He loves me too."

"It's a lot for two young people."

"Do you think this is real, Mama? Or is it just us being stupid kids?"

Crystal sighed, thinking about her answer. "Love is always real, sweetie. Your love right now is as real as if you were thirty and fell in love. It's not the love that's not genuine, it's the people."

Tamira sighed, considering her mother's words. "I wish I knew how this would turn out. It's so scary."

Crystal let out a knowing laugh. "Oh no, you don't. Never wish for that. However, it turns out, knowing will ruin what you two have right now." She lifted her daughter's chin and looked into her eyes. "I know this is going to sound weird coming from me, all things considered, but don't worry about the future so much. You're young and in love. That's the best thing in the world. Enjoy it. Experience it." Crystal wiped a tear from her cheek. "Live it, sweetie. Some day you might not have it anymore."

"Oh, Mama, that's what scares me so bad." Tamira fell against her mother's chest, crying.

"I know." Crystal stroked her daughter's hair. Tamira was such a strong, independent girl that she sometimes forgot that she was still young and inexperienced in so many ways.

She closed her eyes, and her mind went to her own relationship with Tamira's father. How many days had she wasted with worry? Too many. They were days she could never have again, and she'd wasted them.

"Tamira, I wanted to keep you safe. That's why I hid you from the world, but in doing so I made you feel like you weren't this amazing girl that you are. You're beautiful and brave and strong, and I tried to hide you. I'm truly sorry for that."

"It's okay, Mama. I know you just wanted to keep me safe."

"But to what end?" Crystal hugged her daughter. "You aren't me. You're young and need to experience life. It's dangerous, but it's also wonderful and amazing. I robbed you of so much."

"You did what you thought was right, and for that I love you, Mama," Tamira mumbled sleepily.

Crystal looked down at her daughter. Her eyelids were getting heavy. She stroked her hair gently, smiling. It had been a long time since Tamira had slept in the bed with her.

She held her daughter until she fell asleep, mumbling something about Damon. She tucked the covers around her and switched off the light. Crystal laid in the dark listening to her daughter's slow, rhythmic breathing and prayed that Damon was strong enough to bear the weight of dating her daughter.

Crystal yawned as she plodded sleepily down the stairs. She'd woke early and the worry machine in her mind roared to life as soon as her eyes opened. Tamira was experiencing some of the things that average girls took for granted. Unfortunately, not all those things were good, or safe.

As she passed the front door, movement in one of the sidelights caught her eye. She stopped, pulling the curtain aside. Her brow furrowed when she saw Damon sitting on the small stoop outside their door.

As she watched, he sighed and put an elbow on his knee, and propped his chin on it. How long had he been there, she wondered? Her hand started toward the knob, then she stopped, remembering that she didn't have the bandage for her cheek.

She sighed as she watched him. He was a nice young man, and she was happy for Tamira. Her daughter was happy, and it was because of him. She closed her eyes, considering a decision. When she opened her eyes, he'd switched hands and had his chin propped on the other.

He had settled in for a long wait, committing himself to be here for a while. Crystal smiled. He'd made her decision for her.

Crystal ran her fingers along the fresh bandage tacked on her cheek and opened the door. "You want some coffee?" she asked, startling Damon.

He leaped to his feet and turned to face her. "I'm sorry, Mrs. Brannigan. Did I wake you?"

She looked at him over her cup, one arm folded across her pajamas. "No, but you did surprise me a little bit. You wanna come in?"

"Uh, I can, if you want. Or I could just wait here."

"Tamira is still asleep. We were up late." She sipped her coffee, watching him over the cup. "Talking about you."

Damon looked away, blushing.

"Don't worry, it was good. Come on in before somebody calls the cops on you for lurking about like the Boston Strangler."

Damon smiled, remembering that Tamira had called him the same thing. Like mother, like daughter, he thought.

Crystal poured Damon a glass of orange juice and delivered it to the table. The morning sun streamed in the windows of the breakfast nook, soaking him in light. He was quite handsome, and she could see why Tamira had fallen for him. He had an unassuming air about him that was attractive, but also a quiet strength that was reassuring. He was comfortable with who he was, but not arrogant, and he was mad about her only child.

"What were you doing on the stoop?"

Damon wiped condensation from the glass in front of him, embarrassed. He'd awakened early and couldn't stop thinking about Tamira. "I don't know," he shrugged. "I just thought I'd see if Tamira was up."

"Traditionally, people ring the doorbell."

"I knocked a couple of times. I didn't want to ring the bell in case you guys were still asleep. I didn't want to bother you."

"So, you were just going to sit and wait for her to wake up?"

Damon shrugged. "I don't know. I guess from your side it seems kinda creepy. I'm sorry." He looked at his glass and sighed. "I'm not a weirdo, I promise."

Crystal smiled. "No, it's not creepy, and no one said you were a weirdo. I think it's sweet."

Damon blushed again. "Can I, uh, ask you something?"

Crystal sipped her coffee, eyeing him over the cup. "Sure, kiddo. Go for it."

"Does Tamira like me? I mean, has she said anything?"

Crystal chuckled softly. "She's my daughter, I could never tell you what she tells me in confidence."

"Yeah, I guesso. I shouldn't have asked. I'm sorry."

Crystal smiled. "But she has mentioned that you make her want to throw up."

Damon's head shot up, staring at her with wide eyes. "Really?"

"Relax, kiddo," she said with a laugh. "In a good way." Crystal reached across the table and patted his arm. "You know she likes you, Damon. You don't need to hear it from me."

Damon shrugged, a smile sliding across his face. "Good, because I like her too."

Crystal smiled. "I know you like her, and so does she."

He dropped his gaze to the glass in front of him, blushing again. "Mrs. Brannigan? Can I ask you something else?"

She sipped her coffee, nodding.

Damon rubbed the back of his neck, looking everywhere in the room but at her. "So, there's this school dance coming up."

"I believe Tamira mentioned that." Her pulse quickened. Was he going to ask Tamira to the dance, or was he going to present an excuse for not taking her?

"Well, I want to take Tamira." He looked up at her and swallowed hard. "Now, I know you might not like the idea, but I want to assure you that I will do everything in my power to make sure she's safe. I know you might think it's an unreasonable risk, but it's kind of a big thing. I mean, we're a couple, you know. We're dating, so I want to go with her."

"Have you asked her yet?" she asked, knowing the answer.

"No. I thought I'd talk to you. That way if you said no, I could plead my case. If you still said no..." he trailed off, thumbing the glass.

"It's not my question to answer, Damon. You ask her to the dance, and we'll figure things out after that. Being asked is a big thing for a girl, you know." She nodded at him. "Even if you are dating."

"Okay." Damon sighed. "Thank you."

Crystal sipped her coffee, watching him. This boy, she thought, was willing to sit on the stoop just to be close to Tamira. How long would he have waited? Her heart swelled when an answer came to her. Probably as long as it took.

He was mad about Tamira, that much was obvious. But he was young, and she wondered if he fully grasped how dangerous the world was for her daughter. Tamira told her that she showed him the chip on her hip, but that was a minor injury and easily dismissed.

"Damon, I know Tamira told you about us."

"Being glass and all? Yes. I still don't understand all of it though."

Crystal nodded. "I don't know if you grasp the totality of what that means. You know she can break, right?"

Damon nodded. "She told me."

"And if we do break, there's no fixing it."

"I know. To be honest, it scares me to death. More than it does her, I think."

Crystal nodded. "It probably does. She's more adventurous than I was. I took it to heart when my mother cautioned me. Tamira doesn't." She clicked her fingernail against the cup nervously. She needed to make him understand what she meant. She needed to be sure he understood that "breaking" wasn't just an abstract idea. It was a reality they faced every day.

She sighed and closed her eyes as her hand went to her cheek.

Damon's eyes narrowed as a field of small, individual dots of light suddenly appeared on the wall next to him.

He stared at them, watching them rise and fall rhythmically. He lifted his eyes slowly, following the dizzying array up the wall and onto the ceiling. He traced them across the ceiling, then dropped his eyes to Crystal. She stared back at him with blue eyes set afire by the morning sun.

His eyes darted to the fissure on her left cheek. The sun struck the patch of irregular prisms that filled the opening, resembling a field of diamonds, touching off the display on the wall. She moved slightly, sending spears of light reflecting toward him. He squinted but didn't look away.

Damon swallowed, then looked back at her eyes. A smile tugged at the corners of his mouth. "You are as beautiful as Tamira said."

Crystal closed her eyes, quietly drawing in a deep breath. Only her former husband and Tamira had ever seen her break. "I assume she told you I didn't have a mole removed."

Damon nodded sheepishly. "Don't be mad at her, please."

Crystal shook her head, sending the array of reflections in motion along the wall. "I'm not mad."

Damon looked around the room, his eyes wide and his mouth slightly agape. "This is amazing. That's so cool."

"It's not amazing, Damon. It's a break."

Damon shrugged. "I know, but it's still beautiful."

"I'm broken, kiddo. I can never be fixed. I'll be like this for the rest of my life."

"Broken?" he asked, shaking his head. "You're not broken, Mrs. Brannigan. You have a break, but you're not broken."

"There's not much difference, Damon."

He slid from his chair and rounded the table. Standing beside her, he held out his hand, catching a few of the reflections in his palm. "I know you think there's not, but there is. I know it's not me, and that I can't even begin to understand how you feel, but I think you're beautiful."

"You're sweet," she said smiling. "Thank you."

Her smile shifted the reflections on his palm. "You're just like Tamira. She doesn't think she's beautiful, but she is. Just because the world can't see how beautiful you are, doesn't make it any less true."

"Oh, Damon. If only the world was full of more people like you." She put the bandage back over her face with a sigh.

"It may not matter, maybe you think I'm just a kid and all, but I don't think you're broken."

"Damon, I wanted to show you what can happen to her. Would you still think Tamira is beautiful if this happened to her face, or worse?"

"I would," he shrugged. "I don't love your daughter because she's perfect. I love her because she's who she is. A chip or even a break wouldn't change who she is. Not to me."

"Unfortunately, we don't live in a world that thinks the same way. Could you imagine if I went out in public without covering my face?"

Damon shrugged. "Maybe the world needs to know how amazing you both are. Being made of glass is pretty spectacular."

Crystal took his hand and squeezed it. "You're a sweet kid. No wonder my daughter is head over heels for you." She looked up as a toilet flushed upstairs. "And speak of the devil," she said with a smile.

Tamira staggered into the kitchen rubbing her eyes. "Mama?" she asked sleepily. "Why are you up so early?"

"We have company for breakfast," she answered, refilling her coffee cup.

Tamira's head jerked up and her eyes flew open as she looked around the room. When she saw Damon, she smiled for an instant, then remembered she'd just gotten out of bed. She'd slept in a pair of pink running shorts and a baggy tee-shirt. Her hair hung about her shoulders in a tangled mess.

"My God, Mama," she protested, taking a step back, putting the refrigerator between her and Damon. "A little warning would be nice. Her hands went to her hair, combing her fingers through it frantically. "Thanks."

"What was I supposed to do? He was sitting on the stoop when I got up. I couldn't just leave him out there." She looked at Damon and threw him a wink. "I'm taking my coffee outside. It's shaping up to be a beautiful morning."

Tamira did the best she could with her hair and smoothed her tee shirt as she stepped back into the kitchen. Damon was coming around the table, smiling like he'd won something.

"Good morning, beautiful."

"Good morning," she mumbled, shaking her head.

He took her hand as she tried to fix her hair again. "My god, you're beautiful."

"Stop," she said, dropping her eyes to the floor.

"I have something to ask you."

"Okay," she said smiling.

He lifted her chin gently. "Tamira Brannigan," he said, staring into her sleepy eyes. "You are the most beautiful girl in the world."

"Hardly," she scoffed. "I'm afraid to even see myself in the mirror. I must be a mess. I didn't know you were here."

"I know. It's fine. You're beautiful and I'm crazy about you, you know that. But, uh, will you go to the Homecoming Dance with me?"

Her eyes flew open wide, and a smile swept across her face. "Yes!" Tamira squealed, throwing her arms around him. She kissed his lips. "Yes, yes, yes."

Damon held her, staring into her eyes. "I love you so much."

She dropped her gaze, pushing her hand over her hair. "I love you too." She shook her head and laughed. "This'll be some memory. Me looking like a witch the first time you ask me to a dance."

His eyes searched hers as she looked at him and a smile came to his lips. "You're so beautiful. I just can't..." he trailed off as his voice faltered. "I just can't imagine my life without you in it. I don't want to even try."

Tamira slid her arms around him and laid against his chest. "Is that why you're sitting outside my house on a Saturday morning?"

Damon shrugged. It was his time to be embarrassed. "I just wanted to be close to you."

Tamira drew back and looked at him. "Were you really sitting outside? I thought mom was kidding."

Damon shrugged, looking away. "I woke up early and I couldn't stop thinking about you. I wanted to ask you to the dance, but I wanted to see if it was okay with your mom."

Tamira laid back against him, "What'd she say?"

"She said you could go."

"Really?" Tamira asked. Her lips were pursed tightly, and her brow furrowed. "If I'd asked her, we'd still be fighting about it."

"Well," he said grinning as he slid his hands to her hips. "I guess I just have a way with you Brannigan women."

Tamira planted a quick kiss on his lips. "You must, because she likes you, and I can't get enough of you." She stared into his eyes for a moment, smiling, as her mind started going over the preparations that had to be made.

Her eyes flew open suddenly when she realized that she only had two weeks until the dance.

"What?" he asked.

"Oh God, I've got so much to do! I have to find a dress and make an appointment for my hair." She tore from his grip and ran to the back door, flinging it open. "Mama!"

Crystal Brannigan picked up her cell phone from the table in front of her and waved it at her daughter. "I'm already on it. I just got you in with my stylist. We can start looking for dresses later on today."

Tamira ran to her and threw her arms around her shoulders. "Isn't it just wonderful?"

Crystal smiled through her trepidation. Her daughter's unbridled joy warmed her to her core, but there were also so many unknowns. Unknowns that could be very dangerous for her. Dangers that the veil of her emotions might hide. Until it was too late.

She trusted Damon, but it was everyone else who'd be at the dance that worried her. The world was a harsh place, especially for a girl like Tamira.

Chapter Sixteen

Tamira gasped when she stepped in front of the mirror. The dress was a lavender strapless, with intricate beadwork on the bodice that faded into sheer fabric that ended at the knee, and it fit Tamira like it was made for her. She ran her hands across the beadwork, smiling.

"You look stunning."

Tamira looked at the reflection of the woman standing behind her. Evangelina Witten, the owner of the boutique smiled at her.

"You have the perfect figure for dresses like this," she added, making slight tweaks to the dress. "It hangs on you perfectly."

"I like it," Tamira said, turning to look at her profile in the dress. "It's beautiful."

"You're a very pretty girl, Tamira. It's a lucky boy who gets to dance with you in this dress. You and this dress will definitely make a statement."

Tamira's excitement faded slightly. "I'm not sure if I'm a 'make a statement' kinda girl."

"Nonsense. Every girl dreams of having that perfect night. I take it you have a young man taking you to the dance?"

Tamira smiled. "Yes."

"Of course you do. We also have a tie that he can wear that perfectly accentuates the dress. You'll be a beautiful couple." She tugged at the hem of the dress.

"Trust me, this dress won't stay long. There have already been three girls trying it on. Luckily for you, they didn't have the figure to get it on." A slight chuckle escaped her. "Well, not and get it zipped too."

"It is a beautiful dress." Tamira smiled at her reflection. "I think it's the one."

Crystal looked up at the sound of a woman clearing her throat. She followed Angelina's sweeping gesture and found her daughter. Her breath caught in her throat when she saw Tamira. The dress was beautiful, and so was she.

"Oh my God," she gasped, going to her. "It's perfect."

"Isn't it though?" Tamira asked, beaming.

The two women flanked Tamira as she looked in the full-length mirror. "Your daughter is very beautiful, Mrs. Brannigan. This dress was made for her."

"Thank you so much for all your patience and help." Crystal looked at her daughter's smiling face. "Of course, we'll need shoes and any other accessories you can suggest."

"Naturally. It's been a pleasure-" She looked back as one of her employees entered the showroom.

"I'm sorry to bother you, but your three o'clock is here."

Angelina checked her watch. "Tell her to wait. She's a half hour early." She turned back to Tamira, squeezing her shoulders. "I wish every young lady were more like you. This next girl is insufferable. She's been in here twice already. She's tried this dress on both times." She spared a glance over her shoulder and leaned in. "It didn't fit her either time, and I'm sure it wouldn't today either."

Tamira stiffened when she heard Rachel Parson complaining loudly from the front of the store. A knot tightened in her stomach. She closed her eyes and groaned.

"See what I mean? Ugh." Angelina shook her head. "Do you know her?"

"Unfortunately, yes," Tamira said nodding to Angelina's reflection.

"I'm sorry. If you don't mind, I'll hand you off to Stephanie. She'll take care of anything you need." Angelina bowed out and hurried off, leaving them alone.

"Is everything alright?" Crystal asked.

Tamira rolled her eyes. "That girl," she nodded toward the complaining voice. "That's Rachel Parson. She's from school."

"She sounds delightful," Crystal replied with a grimace.

"About as delightful as a poke in the eye," Tamira said with a laugh. "She's the most popular girl in school." She cupped her hands in front of her breasts a few inches from her own. "The boys can't get enough of what she has."

Crystal laughed. "Well, she missed out on a beautiful dress." She hugged her daughter from behind, looking at her reflection. "My God, Tamira. You are stunning."

Tamira blushed. "It's the dress."

"No. It is a great dress, but you've grown into a beautiful young lady, and I almost missed it." Crystal shook her head, sadness blanketing her face. "I'm sorry."

"You didn't miss anything, Mama." Tamira looked at her mother in the mirror and smiled. "Nothing that mattered anyway."

Damon scratched his head with the tip of his pencil as he watched Tamira. Sitting side by side on the floor in front of the coffee table in her sitting room, they were supposed to be doing homework. He was having trouble keeping his eyes on the paper in front of him.

She'd pulled her hair into a ponytail, revealing a slender neckline. Her eyes sparkled in the light as they darted back and forth across the textbook in front of her. Her brow furrowed slightly, then released. She moved to the notebook beside her and began to write. Her hand held the pencil in a delicate grasp, moving effortlessly across the page. Her script was easy and fluid.

His eyes washed over the smooth, fair skin of her face, caressing the gentle features of her jawline. My god, he thought. You are so beautiful.

Tamira looked up suddenly, catching his gaze. "What?" she asked, a smile parting her lips.

"Nothing." Damon turned his attention back to the book in front of him.

Tamira smiled, then went back to work. She loved catching him looking at her. Every time solidified the truth that all this wasn't a dream.

Damon's eyes went back to her as she worked. There was a realness to her that he couldn't escape. It pulled at him constantly, making him want to touch her. His chest swelled with emotions he didn't fully understand. His eyes found her lips, turned down ever so slightly at the corners, and he wanted nothing more than to kiss them.

Tamira threw a glimpse at him, catching him staring at her again. She leaned slowly toward him, putting her head on his shoulder as she finished writing.

"You know," she said quietly, "We're supposed to be doing our homework."

"I know. I am," he lied with a smile.

"It doesn't look like it."

"I'm studying my favorite subject, you."

Tamira laughed. "Wow. That was corny. Did it ever work back in Indiana?"

Damon laughed. "I never tried it. Actually, I just made it up."

"You're making it hard to keep my mind on my work."

"Good." He took her hand in his. "I could look at you all night. You've trapped my eyes, Tamira Brannigan."

Tamira blushed as she sat up. "Thank you, but we both need to study. There's a test this week."

"I know. I can't help it. I look at you and my eyes won't let me look away." He reached out and caressed her cheek. "I've never seen anybody as beautiful as you."

Her eyes searched his face and she smiled. "Damon Kennedy, you act like I'm the prettiest girl in the world, and I know I'm not."

"To me you are."

"I'm glad you think so." She smiled at him, as her thoughts turned to the dance. Her smile faded quickly as her mind shifted gears, turning to Rachel and the dress.

"Is everything okay?"

Tamira shrugged, watching her fingers fidget with her pencil. "Do you ever just wish it could just be us? I mean, no school, nobody else. Just us?"

Damon nodded. "All the time. I wish I didn't have to go home, or that we didn't have different classes, or even have to sleep for that matter."

"Well, I do like my sleep."

"You know what I mean," he said, nudging her playfully with his shoulder.

"I do." She smiled, rubbing his arm. "Yesterday, when mom and I were dress shopping, Rachel Parson came in. She'd tried on the dress I bought, but it didn't fit her."

Damon shrugged. "It's not hard to see why."

Tamira pursed her lips, squinting her eyes at him in admonition. Of course, he'd noticed Rachel's figure. It was hard to miss. She just didn't like him referring to it. "Anyway, since then I've had this knot in my stomach expecting some big showdown with her over the dress. You know."

"I wouldn't sweat it. She'll probably just make her mom buy her a more expensive one."

"Maybe, but now, as the dance gets closer, I'm getting nervous. I mean, I'm nervous anyway, but now it's worse."

Damon took her hand in his. "I know all this is new and scary for you. People can be mean."

"It was easier when I just stayed home and was invisible."

"I'm sure it was, but were you happy?"

"No. I was miserable." Tamira looked down at their hands. "I'm so happy now, though. I'm just scared something will ruin it."

"Look, Tamira, there's always going to be people like Rachel or Brittany or Easton. They're either self-centered jerks or miserable, rotten little apples with shiny outsides. They like making other people miserable too."

"But why? Why do they always have to be that way?"

Damon shrugged. "They're mean girls, mean people. Maybe they're insecure, maybe they got dropped on their heads as babies. Who knows?"

Tamira sighed heavily, closing her eyes. "I just don't want them to ruin the dance for you by causing a scene or something with me."

"If you're there with me, there's nothing that can ruin it for me."

Tamira propped her elbow on the table and rested the side of her head on her hand. "I hope not," she said, her eyes searching his. "I'm sorry I'm not a more popular girl. If I were, you wouldn't have to go through this kind of stuff."

"Stop it." Damon put a hand on her shoulder. "I fell in love with you. That includes you being a glass girl, it includes your past, it includes your quirkiness, everything. It's all part of who you are and that's who I want to be with."

Tamira forced a smile. "Your life might be easier if you were with someone else."

"Tamira, I sat here watching you do homework for five minutes straight like I was watching a blockbuster movie. The way your eyes moved, the way you crinkled your forehead, the way you hold a pencil, the way you move. I loved every second of it. Not because you were popular, but because it was you. I can't take my eyes off you. If you ever went missing, I could tell the sketch artist guy exactly what you look like."

She laughed. "Stop."

"Nope. I'm never going to stop telling you how beautiful you are."

Tamira blushed, dropping her gaze. "How did I ever get so lucky?"

Damon leaned closer. "I ask myself the same question every single day. I'm the lucky one, Tamira Brannigan." He pressed his lips to hers.

Tamira's tension fled her body the instant their lips met, and her body melted beneath his touch. Her skin reacted to his fingertips, breaking out in goosebumps as his hand slid around her. Her heart raced as he pulled her closer, his lips kissing her hungrily.

Crystal Brannigan stopped suddenly in the doorway of the sitting room and cleared her throat. The young lovers leaped apart and Tamira grabbed her pencil.

"Hi mom," she said innocently.

Crystal looked back and forth between the two, then settled on Tamira. "How's the studying going?"

"Good," Tamira said, her voice coming out in a squeak. She cleared her throat. "It's going good."

"Are you guys studying math-" she shifted her gaze to Damon, "-or anatomy?"

Damon's eyes fell. "I'm sorry. It was my fault."

Tamira looked up at her mother and put her palms together in a praying motion. She mouthed the word "please", begging her not to make Damon go home.

"Okay then," she finally relented. "Just make sure there's less of that and more studying going on." She turned to leave but stopped and looked back at them. "I'll be back."

"Good going," Tamira whispered as her mother left the room.

Damon shrugged, smiling. "It was worth it."

A smile slipped across Tamira's lips despite her attempt to stop it. "Yeah," she said. "It totally was."

Chapter Seventeen

"Oh boy."

Damon followed Tamira's gaze and found Rachel Parson standing on the landing outside the school. The white dress she wore accentuated her ample curves and probably pushed the boundaries of the dress code. Her usual crew of girls formed a semi-circle behind her, their arms crossed in front of them. Every one of them was watching Tamira.

"This should be fun," Tamira whispered.

"You know you're going to have to stand up to her." Damon squeezed her hand. "You got this."

"I know," she sighed. "But I can't get into anything physical. Not even a push."

"I won't let it come to that."

"Please don't let me fall down the steps. That scares me more than Rachel does."

He slid a hand around her waist as they mounted the steps. "I got you," he whispered. "It'll be okay."

Rachel's glare fell on Tamira as she climbed the steps, following her to the landing. "So, I hear you've been dress shopping?" she asked, stepping in front of them. She put a hand on her hip as she stared at Tamira.

"I bought a dress, yes."

"Why don't you leave people alone, Rachel? Don't you have a teacher to flirt with or something?" Damon asked.

Rachel ignored him, and the chorus of "Ooos" that swept through the crowd. "Yeah, I saw them boxing up the dress you bought. It looked a little gaudy if you ask me. But I guess you need to get attention somehow."

Tamira tugged on Damon's hand, telling him not to respond. She nodded. "They said you tried it on too." Her eyes narrowed slightly as she held Rachel's gaze. A ripple went through the crowd. She considered mentioning what Angelina had said about not being able to zip the dress but decided not to.

"I did, but I didn't like it."

"Good, because I do."

"You would," Rachel replied smugly.

"Why do you even care what I wear? Really?"

Rachel shook her head with a huff as she crossed her arms. "As if." Her crew rewarded her with a chorus of laughter.

"Because having your little friends out here to confront me sure seems like you do care. It looks like you care a lot, Rachel."

"Do you think it matters what you wear? I couldn't care less."

"Good." Tamira waved her hand at Rachel and the crowd of girls behind her. "So all of this is just what? The welcoming committee?"

Rachel shook her head, glaring at Tamira. "Yeah right. Whatever." She threw a dismissive wave as she turned to go into the building. "God, you're so weird." The girls moved to let her pass, then followed her into the school.

"That wasn't too bad," Damon said with a shrug.

"Oh, I'm sure I'll see her again." Tamira shook her head as they made their way through the crowd. "Something tells me that was just a warning shot."

"Watch your back, Tamira. She never goes anywhere without her girls. I'd be careful when I went to the bathroom."

"I don't think she'd try to get physical. It would be too big a risk with the dance coming up. One good scratch and her pictures would be ruined."

"Still." Damon sighed. "Freaking Rachel. What's her problem?"

"Who knows?" Tamira sighed, accepting the consequences of not being invisible anymore. She looked at Damon and smiled, knowing it was worth every second.

"Hey."

Tamira looked up from her work, drawn by the sound of the painfully thin, dark-haired girl leaning toward her from her own desk. Tamira looked at her, smiled, then surveyed the room. The other students were working, and the teacher was scrolling through her phone.

"What?" Tamira asked in a whisper.

The girl offered a slip of paper, nodding for Tamira to take it.

She looked at the girl, then at the paper. When she didn't take it immediately, the girl tossed it onto Tamira's desk and picked up her pencil. "Just thought you'd want to know."

Tamira looked at the teacher. She was still on her phone. Her eyes fell to the folded paper on her desk. She picked it up and unfolded it slowly, reading it twice.

"Rachel is planning something. Watch your back. probably lunch."

Tamira looked at the girl. Her name was Samantha, but everyone called her "Sam". She was nice enough and, like her, she'd suffered at the hands of Rachel Parsons and her squad. In the hierarchy, she wasn't as low as Tamira, but low enough.

She felt a gentle poke on her back. "It's true. I heard it too," came a whisper from Cindy Fields, the girl who sat behind her. She was much higher up the social ladder, but not at the top.

Tamira nodded, giving them both a subtle wave of thanks. She tucked the paper in her pocket with a sigh. She was thankful for the tip, but it was going to make the rest of class torture.

The fact that Rachel was planning a stunt was bothersome. She'd expected something all morning and figured it would come at lunch. That would be the only time she could actually do anything. Both girls had confirmed her suspicions.

Tamira picked up her pencil and wrote, "Thank You" on the top of her page, lifting it so that each of the girls could see it. As she erased the comment, a smile slipped across her face. It was a slight thing, but neither of the girls had gone out of their way to be nice to her, opting like everyone else to just ignore her.

The fact that they'd warned her might have been more of a strike against Rachel than a goodwill gesture for her, but it was something. It was more than either had ever done before, especially Cindy.

Damon slipped into the seat beside Tamira at their usual lunch table. "Hello, beautiful." He looked at the two other girls sitting close by, but not with her. "New friends?" he asked.

Tamira shrugged. "Perhaps I'm becoming less of a leper," she whispered. "They actually spoke to me."

"Look at you." Damon nodded as he began devouring his burger. "Maybe things are changing." He chewed it quickly and washed it down with a long drink of red fruit punch. "Any problems yet?"

"Nope."

"Good. Rachel's probably moved on to torture some other girl."

Tamira shrugged. She considered telling him about the two girls in Science class but decided not to. It was a big thing to her, but he probably wouldn't understand.

"So, didn't you say you had a tie that matched your dress?"

"Yes. It's a soft lavender. Periwinkle, really."

Damon shook his head as he munched on a French fry. "I haven't got a clue what you're saying. I see your beautiful lips moving, but it's like a foreign language."

Tamira rolled her eyes and laughed. "It's a soft, pale purple."

Damon nodded. "Gotcha. So, my mom is on me about picking out my clothes for the dance. I don't know what to tell her. You wanna come by after school and you two get things sorted?"

"Don't you care what you wear?"

"Not really. I'm a jeans and tee-shirt kinda guy."

Tamira laughed. "You guys have it easy. I've got a dress, shoes, hair, makeup, accessories. I'll be busy for hours. You roll out of the shower and throw on some clothes and you're done." When the two girls agreed with her, she nodded. "See."

"Well, you could go like this and be the most beautiful girl there." He nudged her gently with his shoulder. "Am I right?" He looked at the two girls, but they were looking beyond him, their eyes wide with anticipation. He turned and found Rachel standing behind Tamira, holding a can of diet soda.

"Well, well, well. If it isn't the mutual admiration society girls. What brings you lovely ladies to our lowly table?"

"Zip it, new guy."

Damon feigned appreciation, grabbing his chest with both hands. "I feel so privileged. Rachel Partridge knows my name." He knew her name but wanted to make a point.

"You're funny, new guy," she said, throwing him a sarcastic smile. "But this doesn't concern you."

Tamira put a hand on his shoulder as she turned to face the girls. "Can I help you, Rachel?"

"As I'm sure you are aware, I've been voted to the homecoming court."

"I hadn't heard. Congratulations."

"Whatever. Anyway, I just wanted to make sure you and your gaudy dress didn't show up in the background and ruin my pictures."

Tamira forced a smile. "Believe me, I plan to stay as far from you as possible."

Damon looked at Rachel's tight dress and shook his head. "Just in case you're contagious." He turned to Tamira with a wide grin on his face. "I heard skank is the new black this season."

The two girls at their table erupted with laughter, drawing a glare from Rachel. They both stopped laughing immediately and went back to their lunch. She looked back at Tamira and smiled. "Just make sure you keep your distance, weirdo."

"That's the plan." Tamira stared up at Rachel, a mean comment hanging on the tip of her tongue. Although the boys probably appreciated the dress, she saw instantly that it was at least a size too small for her.

"Good." As Rachel turned to leave, she pretended to bump into one of the girls next to her, spilling the soda on Tamira. "Oops," she said, joining the other girls in a chorus of laughter.

Damon jumped up, but Tamira grabbed his hand and pulled him back to the table. She sighed, then pushed herself up with both hands. She looked at Rachel and shook her head.

"Why does it have to be like this?" she asked.

"It's just the natural order of things, weirdo," she said smiling.

Tamira nodded. "Okay. Fine. Just remember, you started all this." She looked at Damon, then picked up his drink. Rachel's eyes widened when she saw the fruit punch in his glass. She put up a hand to stop it, but it was too late. Tamira splashed the drink in her face.

The red liquid poured down Rachel's chest and saturated the front of her white dress. Damon seized the moment of shock to slide between the girls, preventing anything physical from breaking out. The lunchroom erupted and more than a few students had their phones out, taking pictures or recording. By the time Rachel recovered, a teacher was looming over them.

"You bitch!" Rachel spat. "This dress cost over a hundred dollars."

Tamira crossed her arms on her chest so the growing crowd wouldn't see her hands shaking. "Oops," she said. "I'm just so clumsy. I'm terribly sorry."

"Knock it off, ladies. Both of you, to the office. Now."

Rachel glared at Tamira for a second, then stormed off as a smattering of laughter swept through the lunchroom.

Damon looked at Tamira, shocked. She shrugged and shot him a wink as the teacher escorted her away. He looked at the girls who'd come with Rachel then picked up Tamira's water bottle.

"Anybody else thirsty?" he asked with a grin. The girls back peddled and retreated to their table without saying a word.

Rachel pulled her dress away from her body and examined the red stain. The dress was ruined. She wiped her hands on her lap and glared across the principal's office at Tamira.

"You'll pay for this, you weird bitch."

Tamira shook her head but didn't look up. "Why, Rachel? Why does it have to be like this?"

"Because I hate your guts."

"Why?" Tamira looked up. "What did I ever do to you? I've not spoken two words to you since we've been in school."

"Good."

"I'm no threat to you." Tamira sighed. "Look at you. You're the prettiest girl in school, you have a figure the boys can't seem to get enough of. You're popular, you can date any boy you want. What I don't understand is why you even concern yourself with somebody like me."

"Just shut up, weirdo."

"Okay, I'm the weird girl. Big deal. How is that bothering you?" Tamira ran her hands over her hair. "I mean, everybody is jealous of you. Nobody's jealous of me. You won before this thing even got started."

"Whatever."

"Is this about the dress?"

"Just shut up, okay? I'm sick of you."

"You know, I had no idea you tried on the dress. If you want it, take it. I don't care."

"I don't want the stupid dress. It's gaudy anyway."

"Really?" Tamira sighed. "Is that why you tried it on twice?"

Rachel's head shot up, her eyes finding Tamira's. Anger flushed her cheeks. "Shut up, bitch."

"Angelina told me after I bought it. I was there when you came in." Tamira rubbed her forehead, considering her words carefully. "She told me you tried it on twice and couldn't get it zipped. She basically said you were too fat for it."

"She's a hack anyway. Who cares what she said?"

"I don't, but do you want to know something? I could have said that this morning. I could have told the whole school what she said about you and the dress. She's got the most exclusive boutique in town, and she said you were insufferable and fat. I'm sure there are plenty of girls who'd get a kick out of that."

"Who the hell cares what you say?"

"Nobody." Tamira shook her head. "I didn't make fun of you because I don't think it's funny. I think you look awesome. Plenty of boys do too, I'm sure. So that dress didn't fit, big deal. It was a small."

Rachel turned her head, refusing to look at Tamira.

"Another reason I didn't say anything is because I don't hate you, Rachel. Despite all the crap you do. I'm not going to waste my energy hating you. So go ahead, call me names, say stuff about me. I don't care." Tamira sighed as she looked at Rachel. "But I'll tell you one thing. I'm sure you've gone to every dance since grade school, but I haven't. This is my first time being asked and I'll be damned if I let you ruin it for me, or Damon. I don't want to, but if I have to, I'll punch you right in your damned face."

Rachel turned and opened her mouth to speak, but the door opened. The hulking form of the principal walked in and sat behind his desk. He looked at both girls and sighed.

"Anyone want to tell me what's going on here?"

Tamira looked at Rachel, holding her stare. "Nothing."

"Miss Parson?" he asked, turning to Rachel.

"Nothing. We just bumped into each other in the cafeteria. That's all."

"Miss Brannigan, care to elaborate?"

"Nope. That pretty much covers it. Just an accident."

He looked from one girl to the other and shook his head. "Well then, I'm sure we'll be more careful in the future. If there are any more 'accidents', you girls will be looking at a suspension. Am I clear?"

"Yessir."

Rachel stared at Tamira for a moment, then looked at the principal. "Crystal clear."

Chapter Eighteen

Tamira stood in front of the mirror, smiling, as her mother zipped the back of her dress. It was the first time she'd worn it since trying it on and she'd almost forgotten how it made her feel. It was hard to believe the girl in reflection was her. It had to be someone else. The reflection was a beautiful and sophisticated woman, not a gangly, awkward girl.

Her breath caught in her throat as she tried to speak. "Mama," was all she could manage.

Crystal smiled. Looking over her daughter's shoulder, she caught Tamira's eyes in her reflection. "You're the most beautiful girl in the world."

Crystal watched her daughter's fingers dance along the gentle curve of the neckline. As a mother, she'd preferred something that covered her shoulders, but there was no denying that it was a beautiful dress and her daughter looked beautiful in it.

"I hope I don't do something stupid and ruin it." She smoothed the dress over her stomach.

"You'll be just fine. Relax. Enjoy your big night, sweetie."

"You know, all the couples were invited to submit one song they'd like to dance to. Damon told me yesterday that he submitted one."

"Aww. That's sweet. What song did he pick?"

Tamira shook her head. "He wouldn't tell me. Knowing him it's probably something crazy that nobody could possibly dance to."

Crystal laughed. "I wouldn't worry. I'm sure he's got a lovely song picked out for y'all." Crystal sighed. "You look so grown in this dress. You're not my baby girl anymore."

Tamira smiled. "Don't you cry, because then I'll cry, and my make-up will be ruined."

"I'm not going to cry, sweetie. Not yet." She touched the diamond earrings hanging from Tamira's ears. "You like these?"

"I do. They match perfectly."

A sad smile escaped Crystal. The fact that they were clip-on and not pierced highlighted the fact that they were different. Her daughter would never be a "normal" girl, but at least she was getting a chance to try.

Tamira touched her mother's hand resting on her shoulder. "Thank you, so much."

"You're a beautiful young woman, Tamira. I'm just sorry it took a boy to make you see that and not your own mother."

Tamira patted her mother's hand. "You've always done good for me Mama. You were in an impossible situation. I know that now. I owe you everything. I love you so much."

Crystal sighed. "Okay, we'd better get moving. You've got a boy waiting downstairs on pins and needles. I'm sure he'd like to see you too." She watched Tamira turn in the heels. "And God knows it's going to take you half an hour to get down the steps. Please, be careful."

Damon's face flushed instantly when he saw Tamira. His mouth fell open and his grip loosened on the corsage. It fell from his hand, unnoticed, as she dismounted the final steps.

She'd always been beautiful, but tonight she was on a whole different level. Her misty eyes sparkled as much as her dress when she looked at him. He swallowed hard. He was in over his head. How could he possibly dance with someone so beautiful, so perfect?

"Damon," Crystal said, clapping her hands in front of his face "Earth to Damon. Breathe, kiddo. Breathe. We can't have you passing out again." She waved a hand before his eyes, pulling him out of his trance. When he looked at her, she smiled. "I thought we'd lost you there for a minute."

He nodded, turning back to Tamira. "I thought so too." He stepped forward, kicking the bouquet. He bent awkwardly and picked it up before lumbering across the room to her side.

His eyes swept over her again. Her hair was pulled to one side, laying on her shoulder in big, loose curls. The dress clung to her frame, accentuating her thin figure perfectly.

"Do I look okay?" she whispered. "You like the dress?"

Damon nodded, then leaned closer. "All the times before, I didn't know what I was talking about when I said I was overcome with desire. But now." He swallowed. "Now I am." He gently took her by the shoulders and kissed her lips.

"Okay, okay. You two knock it off before I get the hose. We gotta get pictures and y'all still gotta go to his house for pictures. If you don't get on with it, you'll be late to your first dance for Pete's sake."

Tamira laughed as Damon stepped back from her.

"And look," Crystal poked him in the ribs with a finger. "Be careful that you don't get any idea just because it's a strapless dress."

Damon's face flushed. "Yes ma'am. I will. I mean, I won't."

"Mom," Tamira protested.

"And she's not going to be able to walk fast. She's not used to heels, so hold onto her. Don't let her break a leg for crying out loud."

"Mama."

Crystal ushered them in front of the door and raised her phone to take a picture. She paused and looked at him. "And Damon?"

"Yes ma'am?"

"You look positively handsome."

"Thank you," he said, a wide grin breaking out on his face. He put a hand on the small of Tamira's back, smiling as the first flash went off.

"Oh my God," Linda Kennedy gasped as Tamira stepped out of the car they'd hired to take them to the dance. "You look like a princess."

Tamira blushed. "Thank you, I feel like one."

"Wow, kid," his father said, punching Damon in the shoulder. "You're swimming in the deep end."

"Thanks, Dad," Damon replied, nodding. "I think."

"Stop it, Tom. I think he's handsome." Linda straightened his tie. "You two look absolutely magical."

"I still got time to show you guys some of my sick dance moves if you want," Tom offered as he began to dance.

"Mom, can't you control him? Please." Damon asked, putting his hand over Tamira's eyes. "Save yourself. It's too late for me."

"Seriously. When I was your age, I could burn up a dancefloor."

"You mean they'd invented dancing already?" Damon laughed.

"You bet they did, and I was a terror on the dancefloor."

"Wait, didn't you go to an all-boys school?" Tamira asked, laughing. "Who were you dancing with, Mister Kennedy?"

"Oh! Burn!" Damon exclaimed, laughing as he pointed at his father.

Tom Kennedy laughed. "Okay, okay. I get it." He gave Tamira a quick embrace. "I love this girl." He pointed at Damon. "She'll keep you in line, kiddo. Don't screw this up."

Tamira nudged Damon with her shoulder. "Yeah, don't screw this up."

"Okay, it's picture time. C'mon," Linda said, brushing her husband aside.

Damon sighed, dropping his shoulders.

Tamira took his arm and kissed him on the cheek. "Isn't this the best night ever?" she asked quietly.

He nodded as he looked at her, his smile returning. "How can it not be?" He took her hand. "Tamira Brannigan, you're the prettiest girl in the world. I hope tonight never ends." He leaned in for a kiss as a camera flashed.

The sound of people whispering started as soon as Tamira and Damon walked into the gym, pausing beneath the lattice arch to have their pictures taken. The sound moved with them as they slowly made their way across the gymnasium floor.

Tamira felt herself flush. The air around her was suddenly hot and stuffy. People were looking at them and talking as they passed. She couldn't hear what they were saying, but the knot in her stomach tightened.

Damon touched the hand resting on his arm. His fingers caressed it gently, then he laid his over hers. "You okay?" he asked quietly.

"I think so. Why is everybody looking at us? Do I have something on my face?"

"They're not looking at us, Tamira." He shot her a smile. "They're looking at you."

"Me?" she asked, suddenly terrified. "Why are they looking at me?"

He nodded. "People always stare at the most beautiful girl in the room."

Tears welled in her eyes, but she fought them back with deep breaths. She turned to talk to Damon but hesitated as another couple approached.

"What's up, man?"

Tamira stiffened. It was Easton Brooks and his date, Sherlyn Cosby. She caught his stare and offered an obligatory half smile.

"Hey, Easton. How's it going?" Damon asked. Their friendship had been on a steady decline as his relationship with Tamira grew and he'd let it slide.

Easton tugged at the red bow tie around his neck. "Can't say I enjoy this monkey suit." He looked at Tamira, taking her in from head to toe. "Wow. You really look nice."

Sherlyn stepped closer to Easton, blocking his view. She looked over her shoulder, glaring at Tamira.

"Let's go, Easton," she said. "I need something to drink."

As they walked away, Sherlyn bent to Easton's ear, shaking her head as she talked to him. "You can put your tongue back in your mouth now."

Damon laughed, then looked at Tamira. "Wow, and we're off to a roaring start."

Tamira put a hand to her stomach. "I'm so nervous."

He slid an arm around her waist. "Don't be. It's just you and me. None of these people matter. They're not even here."

"I wish." She looked beyond his shoulder and groaned. "Oh God no," Tamira groaned, nodding over Damon's shoulder. "The hits just keep coming. We haven't even made it to the refreshments yet."

When he turned, he saw Rachel making her way toward them. "Good God," he moaned. "Not this crap again." He clutched Tamira's arm, watching Rachel approach in a black, body dress that fit her like a glove. The dress had a plunging neckline, putting her ample cleavage on full display.

"So you did have the nerve to show up after all." Rachel put her hands on her hips as her eyes washed over Tamira.

Tamira nodded. "I told you I would."

Rachel looked at Damon, then swept her eyes over Tamira again. She found Tamira's eyes, holding her gaze. After a moment, her features softened, and she almost smiled. "That dress looks pretty good on you."

"Thanks," Tamira said, smiling. "You look absolutely gorgeous. I wish I had the figure to pull that off so well."

"Thanks." Rachel turned to Damon, hooking a finger behind his tie. She raised her hand, letting the fabric slide between her manicured fingertips. "Maybe we can dance later?"

Damon put an arm around Tamira and pulled her to him. "I think I'll be busy, but thanks, Rach."

"Good answer, new guy." Rachel smiled at Tamira and shot her a wink before turning and sauntering off.

Damon sighed, watching Rachel walk away. There was no denying that she looked good in the new dress she'd found.

"Okay, now. Breathe." Tamira poked him in the ribs.

"What?" Damon asked laughing.

Tamira used his tie to pull him to her. She planted a quick kiss on his lips and smiled. "Remember me?"

Damon laughed. "How could I ever forget you?"

"I think you did for a second there when the cleavage show was going on."

"What?" Damon shrugged. "I didn't even notice. Cleavage? I didn't see any cleavage."

"It's okay. This time." She pulled him with her as she started toward the dance floor. "You're a big oaf, you couldn't help it. But you must be punished by having to dance with me."

Tamira laid her head against Damon's shoulder. "I never knew dancing could make you so tired," she sighed.

"If it makes you feel any better, you still look amazing."

She patted his chest. "You always make me feel better." Tamira sighed, watching the dancers. After the encounter with Rachel, the rest of the night had gone well. A few couples even stopped and talked with them.

"Are you as happy as I am?"

"There hasn't been a day in the last nine weeks and two days that I haven't been happy. You always make me happy."

She looked up at him, surprised that he knew exactly how long it had been since they'd met. Of course, she knew, but guys usually didn't remember stuff like that.

"What?" he asked. "I put it in my phone."

She laughed and leaned against him again. "Can you imagine us in a year?"

"I can. Longer, hopefully."

Tamira smiled. She'd allowed herself to daydream about their future, and even more than once that they were married. It was almost too much to hope for.

Bodies began to move off the dancefloor as the fast song began to wind down. Tamira watched the couples move in the shadows, wondering if any of them had what she had. She hoped at least some of them did, if only for tonight.

Tamira closed her eyes as she clung to Damon. She could feel his heart beating in his chest. It felt like the best thing in the world. She closed her eyes, losing herself in the rhythm of the strong and steady beat. She wanted to sink into him, to become one with his heart and live within him forever.

"Hey," he said as the music began to play. "This is us." He stepped away from her and extended his hand.

The DJ's voice filled the gymnasium. "This one is for Damon Kennedy and Tamira Brannigan. Love Somebody by Lukas Graham. It's a good one ladies, hold onto your hearts."

Damon extended his hand to her further, "Are you going to dance with me or just stand there and look beautiful?"

She felt herself moving but couldn't swear that her feet were working. Damon led her to the middle of the dancefloor, and into the spotlight reserved for couples during their requested song. The song was one of her favorites and she'd played it relentlessly as of late. Alone in her room, she'd play it and dance, pretending Damon was there.

Tears began to stream down her face as he put his hands on her hips, pulling her to him. "How did you know?"

"Know what?" he asked as they began to sway.

"That I love this song."

He kissed her forehead and smiled. "Because I love you. Also, I asked your mom."

Tamira fell against his chest, crying. "Dam you, Damon Kennedy. You're going to ruin my make-up."

He squeezed her to him. "Get used to it, Tamira Brannigan. I'm planning on doing it for the rest of my life."

She leaned on him and closed her eyes as they danced, moving as one. Everything and everyone disappeared as Damon began to sing to her in a whisper. His soft voice washed everything else away. There were no worries, no fears, no past, or future. There was only now, his arms around her, his heartbeat, his soft words in her ear.

Tamira could feel her arms shaking as she clung to him, praying that the song never ended. She wished that Damon really could stop the world like the song said. This is it, she thought. This is where I want to be for the rest of my life.

His body moved against hers. She felt his arms, clenched around her waist, but she couldn't feel the floor beneath her. Tamira opened her eyes and saw streams of glimmering light moving across the darkened bodies that surrounded them. She watched them dreamily for a moment before realizing what they were. The spotlight above them was reflecting off of the beadwork on her dress. Specks of light shimmered throughout the gym, revolving slowly, following them around the room.

As they began the second revolution, her eyes flew open wide, and she gasped. Her hands clutched Damon tightly, holding on. In an instant, she saw her father twirling her mother. They were young and in love. Then he sat her down and she stumbled. She fell and suffered the break that had ruined their relationship and haunted her for the rest of her life.

"Shhh," he whispered. "I've got you."

Damon lowered her slowly, holding tight to her waist. He held her to him as he began to sway in place again. Without speaking, he put a reassuring hand on her back and held her to his chest.

Tamira closed her eyes again and inhaled his scent, and the moment. Her fear vanished as his arms held her. He hadn't dropped her or let her fall. He'd held her, protecting her the whole time. She was safe in his arms. Her life had gone from sad and lonely to being loved perfectly by the greatest guy in the world. It was a love story she'd never dared to even dream but was somehow living.

Her heart belonged to him, and she was hopeless to ever retrieve it, not that she'd ever want to. Someday, she thought, I will look back on tonight as one of the greatest days of my life and it's all because of a boy named Damon Kennedy.

Damon gently lifted her from his chest as the music began to fade. He cradled her chin gently in his hand, looking into her eyes. "I love you more than I ever thought possible."

"Me too," she said, wiping tears from her cheeks. She searched his eyes and found the answer to her question. Yes, he'd planned the spin, just to prove to her that she was safe with him. She wasn't her mother, and he wasn't the one who let her fall.

He gently thumbed tears from her cheeks as he stared at her. "Are you okay?"

Tamira nodded, unable to speak. She was more than okay. She was in heaven.

Damon stared into her eyes, a smile spreading his lips. "Tamira Brannigan, will you marry me?"

Her mouth fell open as his words snatched from her dreamy thoughts. She stared at him. "What?"

"Will you marry me?"

Tamira looked around, for the first time noticing that a circle of people had gathered around them, watching. She looked at Damon, then hurried off the dance floor, dragging him behind her.

"What are you doing?" she asked in an excited whisper.

"Proposing," he said with a smile.

"Are you crazy?"

Damon nodded. "I am."

"Are you serious?"

He nodded again. "I am."

"You're joking. Is this like before?"

"No. I mean it." He took her hands in his.

"But we're just kids. We're fifteen."

"Okay," he said with a shrug. "We can wait a little bit."

"A little bit? You think?" She carefully wiped tears from her eyes with the tips of her fingers as to not ruin her mascara. "You're crazy."

He cradled her face in his hands. "Look, I haven't researched the legality of all this but-"

"Legality?" She put a hand to her forehead, then let it drop to her side. "You are crazy." She shook her head.

"I think we've established that I am. And that it's your fault."

"My fault? How is it my fault?"

"Really?" Damon sighed as he pulled her to him. "You're beautiful and perfect, and smart and funny and amazing. I couldn't imagine not being with you. I think I'd die. Honestly. I mean it." He sighed. "I know we're just kids. We can wait. I just wanted you to know that I want to spend the rest of my life with you."

Tamira fought a smile. "And you want to marry me?"

"Well, I did. After your reaction, maybe I'll reconsider."

"What? Reconsider?"

Damon shrugged. "I was kinda hoping for a different reaction."

"Oh no, Damon Kennedy." She put her arms around his neck. "There are no take backs. You said it."

"Fine then. Answer the question."

She looked up at him and smiled, shaking her head. "Damon Kennedy, on some indefinite day in the future of our lives, yes. I will definitely marry you."

He bent in and kissed her. "I don't have a ring or anything yet."

"No ring?" she laughed.

"Well, it all kinda was spur of the moment. I mean, I've thought about it, but asking just kinda happened."

Her smile vanished. "I gotta say, this thing is kinda falling apart on you, kid. No ring, no date. Not looking good for you, big fella."

"Gimme a break here. I'm fifteen. I've never done this before."

"Well, technically, you have. This is the second time you proposed to me, you know."

Damon laughed. "But this time you said yes, so I'm one and one. Not too shabby."

"I can promise you this, Damon Kennedy. I'll love you till the day I die."

"Well, Tamira Brannigan, I don't think dying could make me stop loving you." He kissed her forehead then hugged her to his chest. "I know it wouldn't. Not even death could stop me from loving you."

"Me or you?" she asked with a grin, one eyebrow cocked playfully.

"What?"

"You said death couldn't stop you, but who's dead? Me or you?"

Damon laughed. "You've been hanging out with me too much. That's a question I'd ask."

"Well?" she asked, her other eyebrow rising to meet the first.

"Me. I mean, it's understood that if you die, I'd still love you. The whole point I was trying to make is-"

"Hey," she interrupted with a smile. "I'm kidding. This is the part when you kiss me."

Chapter Nineteen

Damon balanced the plate of homemade nachos on one hand and pulled the door closed behind him with the other. He carried the food to the blanket Tamira had spread on his parents' deck.

Last night, they'd stayed until the dance ended, and took their time making it home. Emotionally spent, they'd both slept past noon and decided to have a casual night on his deck watching the stars.

"Dinner is served." He handed her the plate, then produced two cans of Coke from the pockets of his cargo shorts.

"Thanks. You're the best." Tamira sampled the nachos and smiled. "Wow. They're good."

"Just one of my many talents, to go along with dancing and singing."

She rolled her eyes. He'd made her swoon last night and was enjoying every second of it. She watched him open a can and sit it beside her before opening his own.

"Is this okay?" he asked. "I could get something else."

"This is perfect," she said smiling. She looked up at the sky. The first stars were just becoming visible in the twilight. "Last night was amazing. I can't stop thinking about it."

"It was pretty awesome. I still can't get over how beautiful you were." Damon laid back on his elbows and she followed suit, looking skyward. "Did you tell your mom?"

"About you proposing? No," she said shaking her head. "But only because she'd probably just think we were silly kids."

"Yeah. I didn't say anything to my folks. I kinda like that it's something we have that's just ours. For now."

Tamira shrugged, her eyes searching the sky. "You know, when I was a kid, we used to lay on a blanket and look at the stars. I have this one vivid memory of me and my mom and dad laying in the yard on a blanket. We were just laughing and talking. It wasn't really anything but it's one of my favorite memories."

He hooked her pinky finger with his as he looked skyward. "It's pretty, like you."

She gave him a quick pec on the cheek. "You're sweet." She smiled and looked at the stars again. "My mom told me she showed you her break."

Damon tensed, unsure how to proceed. "And?"

Tamira shrugged. "She just told me she showed it to you. She said she wanted you to know we could break in other ways than a little sliver."

"That makes sense. She loves you very much."

"I know. And she worries a lot." Tamira sat up with a sigh and wrapped her arms around her knees. "Her mom hid her out for a long time. People knew what happened, you know. How she was turned to glass. She wanted to shield her from that, so they moved here. She was past forty when she had me."

Damon did the math in his head as he stared at her, shocked. "So she's…?"

Tamira nodded. "We age really well."

"Yay for me." Damon high fived himself.

"My dad was her first, and only, love. When the break happened, she didn't know how to handle it. I guess neither of them did."

"That's sad."

"I know. I guess everybody has some baggage."

Damon kissed her on the shoulder. "It's a shame they couldn't work it out."

Tamira nodded, her eyes on the heavens. "Last night, I didn't even know you'd picked me up at first. I already felt like I was floating." She smiled, lost in the memory. "I opened my eyes and saw the lights reflecting off my dress and it was beautiful. It reminded me of the way the light reflects off my mom's face. But when I realized it, I almost panicked."

"I know." Damon sat up and rubbed her back. "I felt you tense up and sat you down."

"And you held onto me."

"I always will."

Tamira smiled, losing herself in her thoughts. "You know," she finally began. "I think the biggest thing that bothered my mom is that before that night, she was flawless."

Damon's hand froze on her back. "What do you mean?"

"She didn't have a flaw on her body. Just pure, creamy white skin without a blemish head to toe."

"Really?" Damon grinned. "That sounds interesting."

"Stop, you pervert. It's my mom."

Damon laughed. "I wasn't thinking about your mom." He reached out and caressed her face with the backs of his fingers. "I was wondering if it was hereditary."

"I'm not telling you. Perv."

"Well, your side butt did look pretty flawless."

"You were supposed to be looking at my chip. Remember? The chip that you broke."

"I thought you said it wasn't my fault."

"Well, for future purposes when you're being a dumb oaf, it's your fault. All other times, less so."

"Oh. I see now."

"You remember how my chip looked?"

"I don't think I'll ever forget your side butt."

"You're impossible," she sighed.

Damon slid closer. "I'm just messing with you. I really didn't see your side butt."

"Thank you."

"Or did I?" he asked laughing. He put his arm around her shoulders. "For future purposes, I did see your side butt and I liked it."

Tamira shook her head as she settled into him. "Anyway, what you *thought* you saw aside, my mother had a hard time with her break. My dad felt terrible. He couldn't handle it. Things got bad between them, and he eventually left."

"That's messed up. Was he a nice guy?"

Tamira nodded. "I mean, I thought so, you know. I was a kid. I remember him reading to me."

"Have you heard from him since?"

Tamira shrugged. "For a few years, I got a birthday and Christmas card with a hundred bucks in it. After a while, they stopped coming." She shrugged, dropping her eyes.

"I'm sorry all that happened the way it did."

"I think it was best. He still loved her, but she was just inconsolable." Tamira paused, thinking. "I think that since Pop Pop made her, and things happened the way they did, she felt like she lost a piece of him." Tamira looked up at the stars for a long time. "She picked up every piece, down to the tiniest sliver. She has them in a tiny little jar in her room."

Damon nodded. "I feel sorry for the guy, you know. One stupid mistake and it ruined everything."

"That's just it. It was my mother's reaction that drove him away. She never forgave him, I think."

"It would be a hard thing to take."

"That's just it. It's not. I've spent my whole life afraid of being broken, or even chipped. I mean, I don't have a speck on me." She nudged him with her shoulder. "Well, I didn't."

Damon drooped beside her. "I said I'm sorry."

"You're not being an oaf right now, so don't be sorry." She poked him in the ribs. "So now, yes, I have a chip. So? I'm not flawless."

"Maybe not flawless, but you're perfect."

She smiled, blushing. "I'm still the same me. I've just got a chip."

"Did you save it?" he asked.

She shrugged. "I did. I guess I'm more like my mother than I want to admit. It's in a drawer at home, wrapped in a piece of felt."

"Can I have it?"

"What?" she asked, pulling back from him slightly.

"Seriously. I'd like to have it. Maybe take it to a jeweler and have a necklace or something made out of it.

If I never took it off, I'd always have you with me. Albeit a piece that I broke, but still." He paused, thinking about his words. "Well, now that I've said it out loud, it sounds a little creepy."

Tamira felt the tears welling in her eyes but didn't try to stop them. She threw her arms around him and fell against his chest. "It's not creepy. It's the sweetest thing I've ever heard." She squeezed him, pressing her body to his. "I love you so much."

"I love you too." Damon thumbed a tear from his own cheek before he lifted her chin. "I know people will say we're just kids, but I love you. Every ounce of my body loves you. I can't think about anything but you for more than thirty seconds. I can't even imagine my life without you in it. I don't want to."

Tamira nodded. "Me too. It's crazy. I mean, with Pop-Pop and mom and the way that whole thing happened and then you moving here and our meeting. That first time we met, in front of the school. When I looked at you, I knew there was something about you. It's like the universe said, okay, Tamira-"

"The universe knows your name?"

She looked at him and sighed.

"I'm sorry. Continue."

"It's like the universe, which knows my name because I'm so freaking cool and also made of glass, said, Tamira, you've been alone long enough. You've suffered long enough. You didn't ask to be a glass girl, but you accepted this crazy, magic, unique thing, and here is your reward."

Damon rubbed her shoulder. "Can I tell you a crazy thing I thought the other day?"

"God only knows but go ahead."

"No, seriously," he began. "Out of the blue, I had this thought about you. It just came to me, and I thought, we will be together for-"

"A hundred years?"

"Yes!" he said, shocked. "A hundred years. That's exactly what I thought."

Tamira nodded as tears began to flow down her cheeks. "I thought the same thing. Not a thousand, not forever, but a hundred years."

Damon put a hand under her chin and kissed her. He enjoyed the heat of her lips on his, the beat of her heart against his skin.

As they kissed, the world fell away. Something began to move between them, an essence, that he'd never felt before. It flowed into him, warming his whole body at once and electrifying the surface of his skin. He felt a weight that hadn't been there before, but not a physical one. It was fearful, but also tender and beautiful.

Tamira inhaled deeply through her nose as her body began to warm. She could feel his lips on hers, his arms around her, but also something else. She could feel him within her. There was a strength where she felt vulnerable, a reassurance where she felt doubt. It was as if a part of her that she never knew was missing finally fell into place.

Damon opened his eyes as she broke the kiss, sitting back. "What was that?" he asked, breathing heavily.

Tamira reached out and caressed his cheek. "Did you feel it too?"

"I don't know what it was, but something happened."

Tamira stroked his cheek with her thumb. There was an intimacy between them that hadn't been there before, a knowing. "It felt like we were melting together or something. Like something was passing between us."

"That's it. That's exactly what it felt like." Damon rubbed his chest with both hands. "I feel different."

"I do too."

"Did I faint or something?"

"I don't think so." She cocked her head to the side, studying him. She broke her gaze and looked down at her hands. Her brow furrowed as she considered her thoughts.

Her hand was trembling as she raised it to his face, stroking his skin gently as tears began to stream down her cheeks. "I don't believe it."

"I know," he whispered.

Tamira smiled. He felt it too, she knew he did. Something deep inside her told her that he felt it. She swallowed hard, keeping her eyes on his.

"All day I've been thinking about you proposing, and I want to be with you so bad. I want to love you, to marry you, to have kids, and grow old with you. I want everything, with you."

"Me too," he said, nodding his head. He closed his eyes and drew in a deep breath. "I feel like I can feel you." He ran his hands across his chest. "It's like you're inside me." He opened his eyes, smiling.

"Last night, when we danced, it was perfect. You made me feel beautiful, and wanted, and loved. You made me feel like I was the only girl in the world, and that was fine with you. You also made me feel safe. I felt completely safe for the first time in my life. Since then,

I've been wishing I could make you feel like you make me feel."

"You do." He took her hands, studying them for a long time. "Do you feel me?"

Tamira nodded as a tear ran down her cheek and dropped onto their clasped hands. "It feels amazing. Why do you love me so much?"

"I don't think I'll ever be able to not love you. I think I've loved you since the day I was born. I know that doesn't make any sense, but it's how I feel. Is that crazy?"

"If it is, I'm crazy too." Tamira shook her head. "I feel like I was made to love you. I mean, all of this, everything, was just a means to bring us together."

Damon looked at her and smiled. "I don't understand what happened, but I'm glad it did."

"I was praying so hard for you to know, to actually feel how I feel about you. I can say it a hundred times, a thousand, but I wanted you to *feel* it. That way there's no room for doubt, ever."

Damon shook his head. "There was never any doubt."

"I know." She smiled. "I can feel that too."

Damon laid back on the blanket. The sky was fully dark now, revealing a myriad of stars. His eyes scanned them, watching as each one twinkled in the darkness.

He pulled Tamira back and she laid beside him, taking his hand in hers.

"Are you a spiritual person?" she asked quietly, looking skyward.

"I didn't use to be, but I think I am now."

"There are things that we don't even understand out there in the universe."

"There are things I don't understand right here on this deck," he said, bringing her hand to his lips. "I mean, I'm desperately in love with a girl made of glass. That still blows my mind."

"You should grow up as one." Tamira sighed. "Do you think some things are meant to be?"

"I think we were meant to be."

"Do you think our futures are already determined?"

Damon shrugged. "If they are, I hope we're together for that hundred years."

"Surely, we will be. Why else would the universe bring us together?"

"I hope so. I think-" The porch light came on suddenly, piercing the darkness.

"Damon?"

"Over here, mom." He sat up and waved to her over the picnic table. "Yeah?"

Her eyes narrowed suspiciously as she looked at him. "Are you okay, sweetie?"

"Yeah. Right as rain."

Her eyes examined him in the dim light. "You sure?"

He gave her a thumbs up. "I'm good."

"Okay then," she said. Her brow furrowed as she stared at him. "It's almost nine. If you're going to walk Tamira home, you better be heading on. It'll be getting late by the time you get home."

Tamira sat up beside Damon. "I was just saying I needed to be getting home. Thanks again for letting me come over."

Linda Kennedy looked at her, then at her son, then back to Tamira. "Yeah, it is getting late, sweetie." She shot Damon another look of concern before smiling at Tamira. "We're getting some prints of you two done. I still love that dress."

"Thanks. Me too."

"Okay, we were just leaving." Damon took Tamira's hand, and they hurried across the deck. They started down the steps but stopped when his mother called him.

"Please be careful sweetie. You got your phone?"

"I got it, mom. I'll be back soon. It's not far."

She lingered at the door, watching them as they hurried down the steps of the deck holding hands.

"Lock the gate behind you," she said.

"I will, mom," he called from the shadows.

"Bye Mrs. Kennedy."

"Bye Tamara. I love you, Damon." She waited for a reply but heard the gate close instead. She switched the light off with a sigh and was about to close the door when the gate opened again.

"I love you too, mom," Damon called.

She smiled, sure that Tamira had made him come back and say that. "Thank you, Tamira," she said as she closed the door.

"What time is it?" Tamira asked as they made the sidewalk. "It didn't seem that late.

Damon checked his phone and showed it to her. "It's eight forty-seven."

Tamira shook her head. "Didn't it seem like time went by fast?"

He took her hand in his. "It always does."

"I think that kiss lasted longer than either of us think." Tamira shook her head. "Do you think a person can want something so bad that it just happens?"

"I don't know." Damon could feel his heart beating fast in his chest, but it felt different now.

Tamira smiled as they crossed the street. "Do you think we both passed out? I mean, you have a history of doing that, but I don't."

Damon interlaced his fingers in hers, the released them. He watched his fingers grip her hand again before raising them. He turned their hands back and forth, examining them. "They feel like they fit together perfectly now."

Tamira nodded. "Has this ever happened to you?"

Damon shook his head as they walked. "Not even close. Nothing like this."

"Me either. I mean, I've never been kissed before, but when you kissed me other times it didn't happen."

"I like it, though," he said with a smile.

Tamira nodded eagerly. "I do too." She laid her head against his shoulder. "A hundred years is a long time, you know."

Damon looked at her and smiled. "Not long enough."

Tamira moaned as fear wracked her. It felt different. It was his fear. She brought his hand to her lips and kissed it. "Let's just enjoy the first seventy-five before we start worrying about the last bit."

Damon agreed and the fear within her dissipated, replaced by a warmth that seeped into every cell of her body. Tamira looked at him and smiled. I love you, Damon Kennedy. More than life itself.

His head jerked around. He was shaking despite the smile on his face. "I love you too, Tamira Brannigan."

She looked at him, her eyes with surprise. She'd only thought her words, but he felt them. "Everything is different now."

"I think so."

She laid her head back against his shoulder as they walked slowly down the street. She could feel him, every breath, every heartbeat.

"I know. It's amazing but scary." He sighed. "I like it."

They walked in silence, allowing themselves to feel each other's emotions. Tamira closed her eyes, letting him lead her. She didn't have to be scared anymore, not with him. Not ever.

When she opened her eyes and raised her head, they were two blocks closer to home. She inhaled deeply and smiled as she looked at Damon. His thoughts were no less intense, but they had slightly altered course. An eyebrow arched as she stared at him, feeling his desires.

He kept his eyes ahead but swept a hand through his hair as she watched. His cheeks blushed with embarrassment. "It's okay," she whispered.

Damon stopped but still couldn't look at her. "I'm sorry. I just wanted..." He shook his head. "I was just... I'm sorry."

Tamira lifted his chin, looking into his eyes. "Really. It's okay. It's natural. It's beautiful. Don't you think I've thought about that too?"

Damon's face flushed again. "I just..."

"Shh. You don't have to explain anything to me." She patted his chest softly.

"I just don't want you to think-" He stopped when the sound of squealing tires drifted down the street. They both turned back, but the street was empty.

"C'mon." Tamira tugged on him, but Damon's eyes were locked on the street. A hand went to the tightness growing in her chest. "It's nothing. Let's get on home."

Damon finally relented and started walking again. He slipped an arm around her waist and threw another look over his shoulder. "I wish we were married already," he sighed. "We wouldn't have to make this stupid walk."

"Wouldn't it be amazing?" she cooed. "To go to sleep and wake up with each other every day. And just lay in bed together."

Damon nodded as a little smile broke out on his lips. "What do you think our first fight will be about?"

Before Tamira could answer another squeal of tires on pavement echoed down the deserted street. It was louder this time. Closer.

Both turned, their hands finding the other's. Several blocks behind them, a car careened onto the street, its rear end fishtailing wildly.

"This guy must be drunk or something." Damon eyed the car, gently edging Tamira further from the road.

"He's something," she agreed. "He's in a hurry to get somewhere too." They watched him until he slid to a stop next to the curb on the opposite side of the street four blocks down. The headlights shut off, but the sound of the engine continued to roll down the empty street.

Damon sighed as he turned and started walking. "Good. It looks like he made it home without killing anybody."

Tamira grabbed his arm, listening intently. "Do you hear that? Is it sirens?"

Damon listened. "It is."

"Do you think the police are looking for the guy?"

Damon shook his head, staring at the car. "I don't know. Let's just get you home. It's getting late." He started walking again but cast a wary glance over his shoulder.

"It's no big deal," she said, rubbing his arm with her free hand. His tension building again, she could feel it in her chest. "Just a drunk. We'll be fine." Her shoulders drooped as another squeal of tires filled the air.

Damon looked at the car, then scanned the area around them. The house next to them had a low wooden fence. He could hop it easily but doubted if Tamira could. The ones on either side of it had hedgerows lining the sidewalk. The second one up had a wide, grassy lawn they could duck into if they had to.

"Let's get up here, just in case he runs off the road." He hurried Tamira along the sidewalk.

"Not too fast," she said. "It's okay. He'll pass by."

The fear was evident in her voice, but it was mingled with the roar of the engine closing in on them. Damon spared a glance over his shoulder as they cleared the fenced-in yard and drew even with one that had a row of hedges.

"Damon!"

He looked down, becoming aware that he was hauling her along the uneven sidewalk with a hand clenched tightly around her bicep.

"I'm sorry," he said. Her fear fell on him like a wet blanket. "I'm sorry." He looked back at the car as it began to swerve. It was still three blocks away. They had time if they hurried.

"This guy's drunk as crap. We have to hurry," he said, pulling Tamira along the sidewalk. "Let's pass this yard and get off the street. Just in case."

"I hear the cops," Tamira said, struggling to keep up with his brisk walk. "Damon, please be careful. Slow down a little. We'll be okay."

Tires squealed in the distance as the police cruiser turned onto the street. Damon glanced back and saw the flashing lights. The driver of the car did too. He gunned the engine.

"Crap," Damon said, looking back as he hurried. "The cops are chasing him and he's trying to get away."

"Damon, stop. It'll be okay." Tamira looked back, shocked at how close the headlights were. Her heart leaped into her throat as the car swerved. It careened off a parked car on the other side of the street and headed straight at them. She shrieked in fear as the one undamaged headlight blinded her.

"Tamira."

Damon's voice sounded distant, drown out by the roar of the engine and the sound of tires screeching on pavement.

"Damon!" she screamed, closing her eyes as the sound of the engine drowned out everything else.

She felt herself being lifted from the ground, then her body exploded in pain. She was flying through the air, twisting, and turning through the darkness. Her screams were everywhere, consuming her. She opened her eyes for an instant and saw darkness, then light, then darkness again. Suddenly she was being slapped and raked by something hard, but not hard as steel. It was wood. The bushes. She was landing in the bushes. Had the car hit her and thrown her into the bushes?

She tumbled for what felt like an eternity, then she landed on something soft and fuzzy. Something? What was it? Grass?

She opened her eyes in a panic, her breaths coming in ragged pants. Her eyes darted back and forth as she lay on her back, afraid to move. There was no telling what was broken, but her body didn't hurt anymore. She called for Damon, feeling for him, but she found nothing but cold darkness.

Flashes of red and blue lights ran across the sky. There was a smell of hot rubber and something else. What was it? Anti-freeze. Yes, from the car. She could smell the engine. It was screaming in her head, but the car had stopped.

Damon! The thought pushed everything else from her mind. Where was he? Was he okay? Had he been hit too?

"Damon?" A coldness began to settle within her body, and she started to shake. Tears streamed from her eyes. "Damon!" she screamed as loud as she could. "Damon!"

The Last Chapter

Crystal Brannigan knocked on her daughter's bedroom door, opening it slowly. Tamira was slumped on the edge of her bed facing the window. The shades were drawn. She looked tired and frail. Spent. She looked broken.

The memory of her time after her face was broken swam into her mind briefly. It paled in comparison to her daughter's grief. She'd never seen such agony from another human being. Watching Tamira's pain hurt her more than anything she thought possible. As bad as she ached, she knew it didn't come close to what Tamira was going through.

Crystal drew in a deep breath, steeling herself. The days had bled together into one long theater of anguish with no end in sight. She longed for something to do, something that would help, but there was nothing anyone could do.

It wasn't just the loss of a boyfriend that Tamira had suffered. It was so much more. It was a loss of everything that made her life worth living. It was promises broken. A life stolen. An end that wasn't supposed to be.

"Sweetie?" She stared at her daughter's slumped form. "Are you ready?" she added quietly. She touched the corners of her eyes with the handkerchief clutched in her hand.

Tamira didn't move.

Crystal closed her eyes, forcing more tears out. "You don't have to do this. Nobody will blame you."

"I have to." Tamira's voice was hollow and distant.

Crystal crossed the room and put a hand on her daughter's shoulder. "You don't have to go."

"I do have to go."

"Okay." Crystal embraced her daughter as she stood. "I'm so sorry."

"It's not fair," she said blankly. Tears began to flow down Tamira's cheeks.

"I know it's not, baby."

"Why?" Tamira exclaimed as she stood. "Why him?" She threw her hands into the air. "Why, Mama! Why did it have to be him?"

Crystal caught her daughter as her knees buckled and helped her back onto the bed. Tamira's whole body shook with violent sobs as she collapsed.

"Why couldn't it have been me?" she cried. Tamira covered her head with her arms, curling into a ball. "Why did it have to be my Damon?"

Crystal's eyes exploded with tears as she hugged her daughter, holding her as tight as she could. The doctors wanted to admit her to the hospital and keep her sedated, but Tamira refused.

"Tell me it's not real, Mama. Please. Tell me this is not happening."

"I wish I could, baby. I wish I could."

"Tell me it's a bad dream."

"I can't, baby."

Tamira pulled her hand free and turned from her mother, pounding the mattress. "No!" she screamed, shaking her head. "It's not real. It can't be real. No! No! No!" Her body convulsed with sobs. "My sweet Damon." Tamira dissolved into tears, crying his name again and again.

Crystal sat on the edge of the bed, holding her only child, crying with her. There was nothing else she could do.

Tamira took a deep breath, slid a pair of sunglasses on, and stepped outside of her house for the first time since the accident.

She recoiled from the bright sunlight and shook her head. Why is the sun still shining, she thought? Doesn't it know?

She took two steps and stopped as her eyes fell on the black car waiting at the curb. She cringed as pain coursed through her body.

"Are you okay?" Crystal asked.

"No, Mama. I'm not."

"Do you want to go back inside?"

Tamira shook her head, letting her eyes drift down to the lawn. The top of the short wall that created their raised yard was littered with hundreds of spent candles. Her eyes swept over them slowly. Although different sizes and shapes, all of them were a soft lavender, similar to the color of the dress she'd worn to the dance.

"The kids from school have been coming by every night, sweetie. They light the candles and just hang out. They're doing it in front of his house too."

"Why?"

Crystal put an arm around her daughter's shoulders. "It's been hard on a lot of people, sweetie. It's all they can do."

Tamira nodded and drew in a sharp breath as another pain struck her. "We'd better go."

Crystal Brannigan stepped out of the car and took a deep breath, preparing herself to help Tamira. She put a handkerchief to her eyes, then looked around. As per her request, everyone was already inside the church and seated. They were late, but they were expected.

The driver kept his eyes to the pavement. "I'm sorry, Ma'am."

Crystal thanked him, then turned back to the car. "Are you sure about this?"

Tamira stepped out of the car. Her hair was in loose strands, and eyes that were vibrant and alive just a few days earlier were vacant. The black dress hung loosely about her frame, noticeably thinner now. She girl before her scarcely resembled the daughter she'd watched grow up.

She was now a woman incomplete. Her story could never be told in any manner that would ever be acceptable to her.

Tamira looked at her mother for a long time, then forced a half-smile. Putting a hand to her cheek, Tamira thumbed the bandage that hid her break.

"Will you do something for me, Mama?"

"Anything, sweetie."

"When you get home will you take that thing off and throw it away. Never wear it again? Let the world see how beautiful you really are."

Crystal put her hand on her daughter's. "I will. I promise."

"You're too beautiful, Mama. Please don't hide anymore."

Crystal closed her eyes, pushing tears from the corners. When she opened them, she forced a smile for her daughter's sake.

"I love you, baby. So much."

"I know you do, Mama. I love you too."

"Are you ready to go inside?"

Tamira drew in a long breath and exhaled slowly before nodding.

The massive sanctuary in the First Baptist Church of Providence, lined with two dozen stained glass windows, was a marriage of structural architecture and elegant beauty. When it was decided that the small church Damon's family attended couldn't hold the throngs of people sure to turn out, the funeral was moved here.

The entire school, faculty, and student body were present. Most of the town, in general, had come as well. Although he was new, and not many people knew him personally, Damon was a kid. People hated to see kids die, especially the way he did.

The room fell silent as the back doors opened. Bright sunlight streamed into the hall abruptly, silhouetting two bodies.

The collective gasp of an entire town sucked the air from the room as Tamira stepped out of the sunlight and into the soft, filtered glow within the church. The heavy doors closed behind her with a noisy clang.

She was the most popular girl in town now. Everybody was talking about her. Everyone knew that she was taking it hard. Nobody thought she'd be able to show up.

Tamira paused long enough to let her eyes adjust. She took a deep breath to steel herself, then removed her sunglasses, handing them to her mother. She closed her eyes and drew in a deep breath before starting down the center aisle.

Her heart stopped, her breath catching in her throat when her eyes swept across the room and fell on the casket. Damon's casket. The rich, polished wood. The brass handles. Damon's casket.

A hushed whisper swept through the crowd. A hand touched her arm, her mother, and Tamira nodded again. She was going to do this. She was going to see him and kiss him one last time. She couldn't *not* do this.

She let the tears roll down her cheeks, uncaring who saw them. He was hers, and she was his. The universe had promised them- she closed her eyes as the thought came to her.

A hundred years.

Tamira bent as an agonizing sob wracked her body. She was heavy and the air in the church was suddenly thick and hot, hard to breathe. As the weight of her sorrow pressed down on her, she dropped to one knee, gasping. Beneath her dress, she felt something crack, but it didn't matter. Not now. Nothing mattered now.

Another collective gasp went up from the crowd as she fell, but she couldn't hear it. She couldn't see them. All that mattered was her and Damon. A hand touched her elbow, but she swatted it away angrily. They left her alone with her pain.

Tamira pushed up off the floor, lifting the thousand pounds of grief that hung about her. She had to see him. She couldn't not see him. Damon was waiting. Her sweet, precious Damon was waiting.

This was her last chance to see him.

Standing, she fought for another breath and started again.

A hundred years, she thought. She stopped again after only a few steps, bending as pain wracked her body. They had been coming in waves since the accident and building in strength. She closed her eyes in a grimace as tears poured from her eyes.

When the pain subsided enough for her to continue, she opened her eyes. They went instantly to the tiny drop laying on the red carpet. It sparkled in the filtered light, shining as it lay there at her feet. As she stared at it, she felt a light tap on her arm and watched another drop fall to the floor. It bounced off her forearm, hit the carpet, and rolled a few inches before coming to a stop near one of the pews.

Tamira drew in another breath and started walking again.

A man in a grey suit sitting on the aisle seat watched her pass, then bent and lifted the drop. He looked at it, rolling it between his fingertips. The woman sitting next to him asked what it was in a whisper.

The man looked at Tamira, then back to the woman. "It feels like glass."

Tamira looked up and found the casket again, focusing on it. He was there, waiting. That was all that mattered. She fought the weight pressing against her and moved forward. Tears rolled down her cheeks and bounced off the front of her dress. They flowed ceaselessly as she walked, leaving a trail of her broken heart in her wake.

She paused when she reached the end of the carpet. It stopped even with the first rows of pews. She didn't have to look. She could feel Damon's family to her right. No one had told her, but she knew there were two empty seats. One was reserved for her mother, and one was saved for her. Her seat was on the aisle, closest to the casket, the seat traditionally saved for the spouse.

Pain ricocheted through her body, touching every inch of her before it abated. She could hear his mother's sobs. The sound echoed the feeling in her chest. Tamira closed her eyes and drew in a deep breath, absorbing as much of her pain as she could stand.

When Tamira stepped forward onto the tiled floor, Linda Kennedy's sobs had stopped, but a murmur was growing among the crowd behind her.

The weight of the pain within her had grown. It was heavy and dark, but she didn't have much further to go. Linda was the woman who brought her, her sweet Damon, she deserved more relief, but Tamira had no more room within her.

A soft tinkling filled the church, like that of a windchime in a light breeze. She knew what it was. She didn't have to look to know that her tears were striking the tiled floor and bouncing in every direction.

They flowed from her like a river, playing the song of her pain and loss for everyone to hear. It was a song sorrowful and beautiful. Haunting. It was the song of love and loss. It was her song.

Another low whisper swept through the crowd, but she didn't hear it. The crowd didn't matter. Just like at the dance, the crowd had disappeared and there was no one but her and Damon.

Damon's voice entered her mind. "They're not looking at us. They're looking at you. People always stare at the most beautiful girl in the room."

She took another step toward the casket, closer to Damon. Her eyes fell on him, and she stopped. The echoes of her tears filled the church in a crescendo of pain.

"Damon Kennedy," she whispered, a thin smile coming to her lips. He was still handsome as he'd ever been. He looked peaceful. Like he was sleeping. She stepped closer.

"Dam you Don Quixote for saving me," she whispered. "You knew I couldn't live without you."

She stepped closer, her breaths coming in labored pants. Whatever had started in her body the moment Damon died was coming to fruition. She'd felt herself go cold that night, but it didn't matter. There was nothing left of her anyway.

His hands were folded over his lap. Hands that fit perfectly in hers. A hundred years, she thought. I should have held those hands for a hundred years.

Her body clenched as another pain exploded within it. Another murmur escaped the crowd behind her. She opened her eyes. The floor beneath her was covered in sparkling fragments of her sorrow.

Gasping for air, she nodded her head. She was tired and nearly spent. She didn't have much time left. Her right knee buckled. She caught herself.

Another gasp went up behind her, but nobody moved. The crowd was frozen by the spectacle.

She pushed herself up and stiffened what was left of her back. Three more steps, she promised herself. Just three more steps.

A hundred years.

Two more steps.

A hundred years.

One more step.

Her legs buckled again, but she caught herself on the edge of the casket. She bent to kiss him but stopped. Tears showered the black tuxedo they'd dressed him in with broken glass. The tiny fragments looked like stars in a midnight sky. Stars they'd watched on their last night together. Stars that had brought them together and broken them apart.

Her eyes went to the sliver of glass laying on his chest. It lay at the end of a thin, black leather necklace. Fine strips surrounded the sliver of her, embracing it tightly. Holding it the way he held her.

She stared at the fragment of herself, wondering how it had gotten there. She didn't know. The last thing she remembered was the warmth of his love spreading through her body. It encompassed her and she could feel him. She could feel his love, and then there was nothing. She was hollow. Cold. Gutted.

A quiet moan escaped her as another pain wracked her body.

She didn't have much time.

Pushing through the agony, she bent over her love and pressed her lips to his, letting the kiss linger.

A hundred years, she thought. A hundred years isn't that long.

She grimaced in pain as she stood. Panting rapidly, she reached out and touched the fragment of herself. Her hand moved to his cheek. She wished she'd kissed him a hundred more times. A thousand. A million, if she could.

"I love you, Damon Kennedy." A gasp escaped her as the first fracture struck. She kept her eyes on his face, her hand on his, as her pants grew faster, heavier. The pain didn't abate. Time was growing short.

She nodded her head. "A hundred years isn't too much to ask for."

A low whisper went through the people on the front row. They were the first ones to hear the "tick" of the fractures. They were soft, muffled by the long black dress she wore, but they pierced the silence like a gunshot. The whispers moved back as she clenched again. A long fracture line slid up the side of her neck. It rolled over her jawline and raced across her cheek, splintering like lightning. The pain was almost unbearable. Almost.

Tears cascaded down her body. Tiny fragments of her fell on Damon, on the floor. At her feet, the tile was white with the pieces of her.

"I love you, Damon Kennedy."

From behind her, someone cried her name. "Tamira!"

The fractures shot across her body before the first usher could stand. The sound of them echoed through the sanctuary. They spread over her in an instant, like a spider web, covering every inch of her.

She looked at his face. She smiled, and then...she shattered.

A note from the author,

To all of those who feel alone, know that it doesn't last forever. To everything there is a season. A season of solitude may be the preparation for a season of togetherness. As in the winter, beneath the cold ground a seed awaits the spring, our souls await our season of growth. Unfortunately, that season too must come to an end at some point. Enjoy it while it lasts.

For more work from this author, please visit his website at: gspressbooks.com

Coming in March 2022 from Moonshine Cove Press:

The Man with no Eyes
by John Ryland

The Facility took almost everything from Doctor Andrew Harkins, including his eyes. What they couldn't take was his unique ability to control every function of his body, from his heartbeat to his hearing acuity. After escaping the Facility, he is determined to use this ability and his genius intellect to find a way to destroy them…if he can survive the merciless open desert that stands in his way.

After Andrew is discovered by Malika, a Yemini woman forced to flee her village after attempting to gain the male-only position of village elder, she agrees to help him destroy the Facility. They traverse the desolate Yemini-Saudi border region to reach the Facility and confront Alain Savon, the maniacal owner. But with gun runners, Facility agents, and the U.S. military chasing them, they may die from a bullet or the desert's heat long before they reach Savon.